TOP SECRET GRAPHICA MYSTERIES

CASEBOOK: VAMPIRES

WITHDRAWN

Script by Justine and Ron Fontes

Layouts and Designs by Ron Fontes

Skyview Books™
an imprint of
WINDMILL BOOKS™
New York

Published in 2010 by Windmill Books, LLC
303 Park Avenue South, Suite # 1280
New York, NY 10010-3657

CREDITS:
Script by Justine and Ron Fontes
Layouts and designs by Ron Fontes
Art by Planman, Ltd.

Publisher Cataloging in Publication

Fontes, Justine
    Casebook—Vampires. – School and library ed. / script by Justine and Ron Fontes ; layouts and designs by Ron Fontes.
p.   cm. – (Top secret graphica mysteries)
Summary: Einstein and his friends use their virtual visors to investigate vampires, ghosts that can act in the realm of the living and need blood to maintain their physical form.
ISBN 978-1-60754-606-1. – ISBN 978-1-60754-607-8 (pbk.)
ISBN 978-1-60754-608-5 (6-pack)
    1. Vampires—Juvenile fiction   2. Graphic novels   [1. Vampires—Fiction
2. Graphic novels]   I. Fontes, Ron   II. Title   III. Title: Vampires   IV. Series
    741.5/973—dc22

Manufactured in the United States of America

CPSIA Compliance Information: Batch #BW10W: For futher information contact Windmill Books, New York, New York at 1-866-478-0556.

CONTENTS

Welcome to the Windmill Bakery

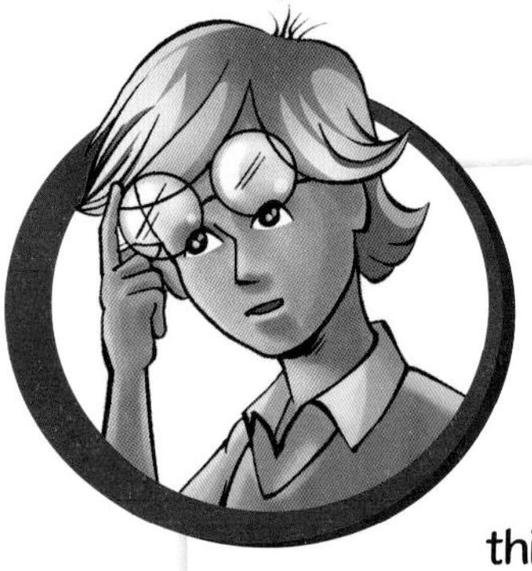

Edward Icarus Stein is known as "Einstein" because of his initials "E.I." and his last name, and because he loves science the way fanatical fans love sports. Einstein dedicates his waking hours to observing as much as he can of all the strange things just beyond human knowledge, because "that's the discovery zone," as he calls it. Einstein aspires to nothing less than living up to his nickname and coming up with a truly groundbreaking scientific discovery. So far this brilliant seventh grader's best invention is the Virtual Visors he and his friends use to explore strange phenomena. Einstein's parents own the local bakery where the friends meet.

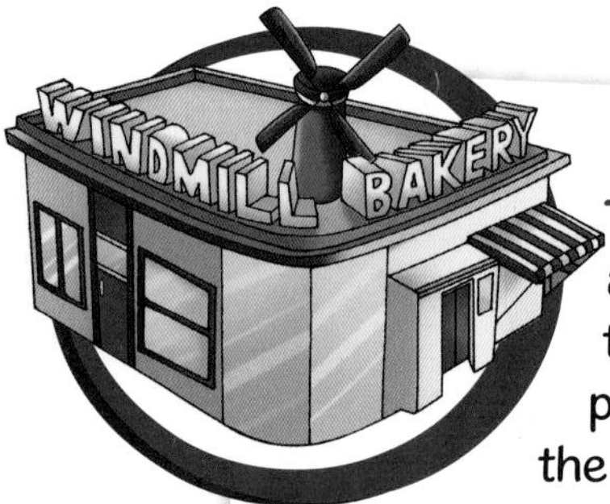
WINDMILL BAKERY

The Windmill Bakery is a cozy place where friends and neighbors buy homemade goodies to go or to eat on the premises. Einstein's kindhearted parents make everyone feel welcome, especially the friends who understand their exceptional son and share his appetite for discovery!

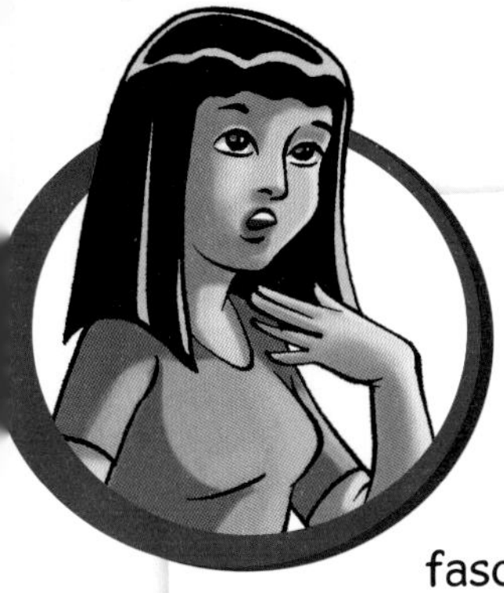

"Spacey Tracy" Lee saw a UFO when she was seven. Her parents tried to dismiss the incident as a "waking dream." But Tracy knew what she saw and it inspired her to investigate the UFO phenomenon. The more she learned, the more fascinated she became. She earned her nickname by constantly talking about UFOs. Tracy hopes to become a reporter when she grows up so she can continue to explore the unknown. A straight-A student, Tracy enjoys swimming, gymnastics, and playing the cello. Now that she's "more mature" and hoping to lose the silly nickname, Tracy shares the experience that changed her life forever only with her Virtual Visor buddies.

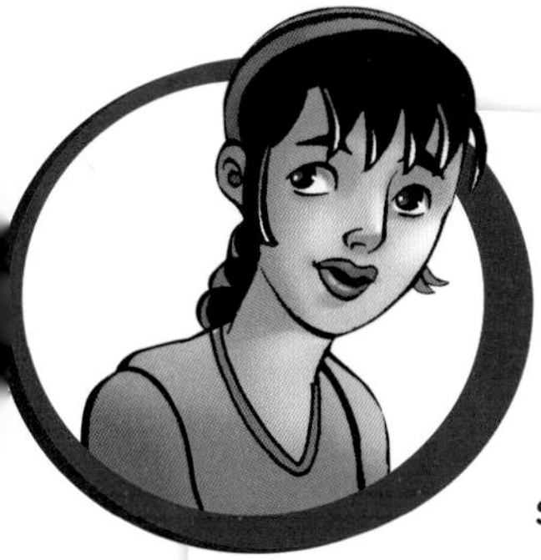

Clarita Gonzales knows that Indiana Jones and Lara Croft aren't real people, but that doesn't stop this seventh grader from wanting to be an adventurous archaeologist. Clarita's parents will support any path she chooses, as long as she gets a good education. Unfortunately, school isn't her strong point. During most classes, Clarita's mind wanders to, as she puts it, "more exciting places—like Atlantis!" A tomboy thanks to her three older brothers and one younger brother, Clarita is a great soccer player and is also into martial arts. Her interest in archaeology extends to architecture, artifacts, cooking, and all forms of culture. (Clarita would have a crush on Einstein if he wasn't "such a bookworm")!

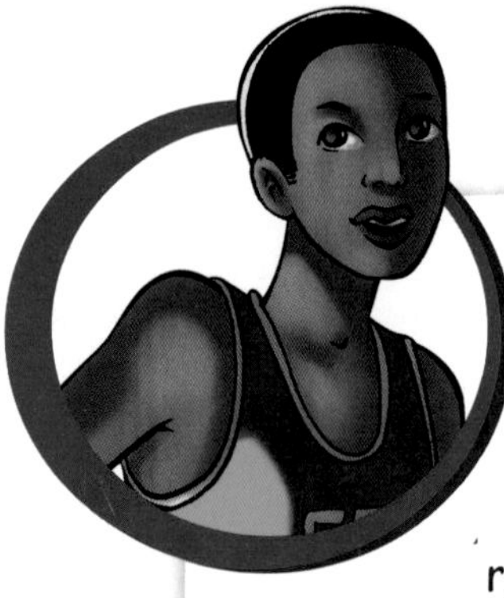

"Freaky Frank" Phillips earned his nickname because of his uncanny ability to use his "extra senses," a "gift" he inherited from his grandma. Though this eighth grader can't predict the winners of the next SUPERBOWL (or, he admits, "anything really useful"), Frank "knows" when someone is lying or otherwise up to no good. He gets "warnings" before trouble strikes. And sometimes he "sees things that aren't there"—at least to those less sensitive to things like auras and ghosts. Frank isn't sure what he wants to be when he grows up. He enjoys keeping tropical fish and does well in every subject, except math. "Numbers make my head hurt," Frank confesses. Frank spends lots of time with his family and his fish, but he's always up for an adventure with his friends.

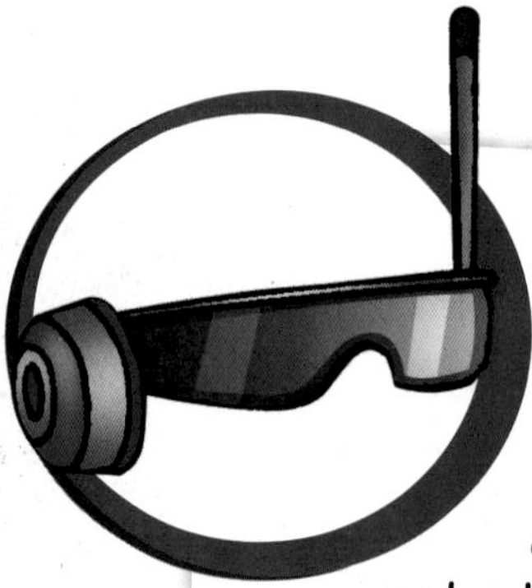

The Virtual Visors allow Einstein, Frank, Clarita, and Tracy to pursue their taste for adventure well beyond the boundaries of the bakery. Thanks to Einstein's brilliant software, the visors can simulate all kinds of locations and experiences based on the uploaded facts. Once inside the program, the visors become invisible. When danger gets too intense, the kids can always touch their Virtual Visors to return to the bakery. Sometimes the kids explore in the real world without the visors. But more often they use these devices to explore the mysteries and phenomena that intrigue each member of the group. The Virtual Visors are the ultimate virtual reality research tool, even though you never know what quirky things might happen thanks to Einstein's "Random Adventure Program."

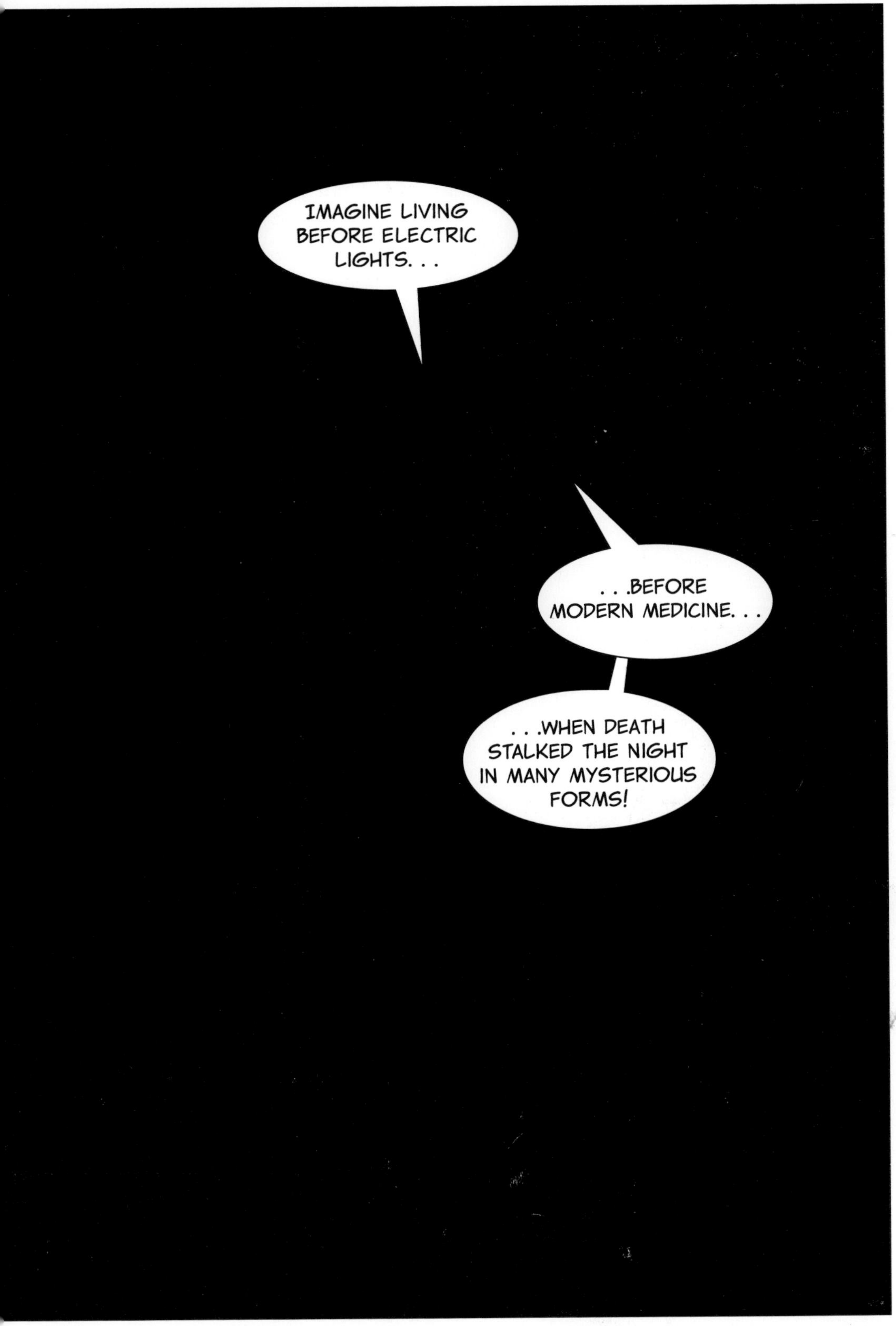
IMAGINE LIVING BEFORE ELECTRIC LIGHTS. . .
. . .BEFORE MODERN MEDICINE. . .
. . .WHEN DEATH STALKED THE NIGHT IN MANY MYSTERIOUS FORMS!

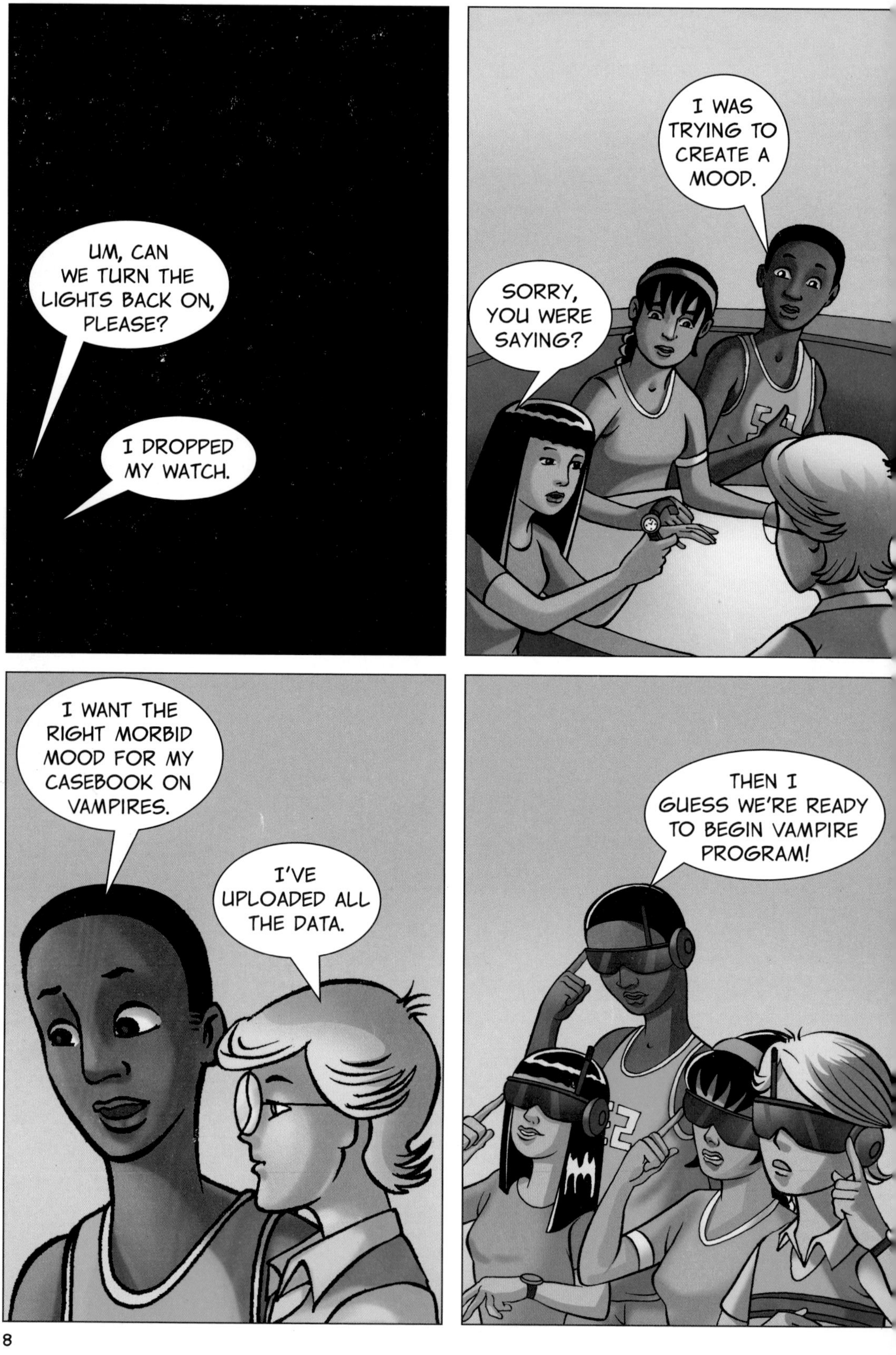
UM, CAN WE TURN THE LIGHTS BACK ON, PLEASE?
I DROPPED MY WATCH.
I WAS TRYING TO CREATE A MOOD.
SORRY, YOU WERE SAYING?
I WANT THE RIGHT MORBID MOOD FOR MY CASEBOOK ON VAMPIRES.
I'VE UPLOADED ALL THE DATA.
THEN I GUESS WE'RE READY TO BEGIN VAMPIRE PROGRAM!

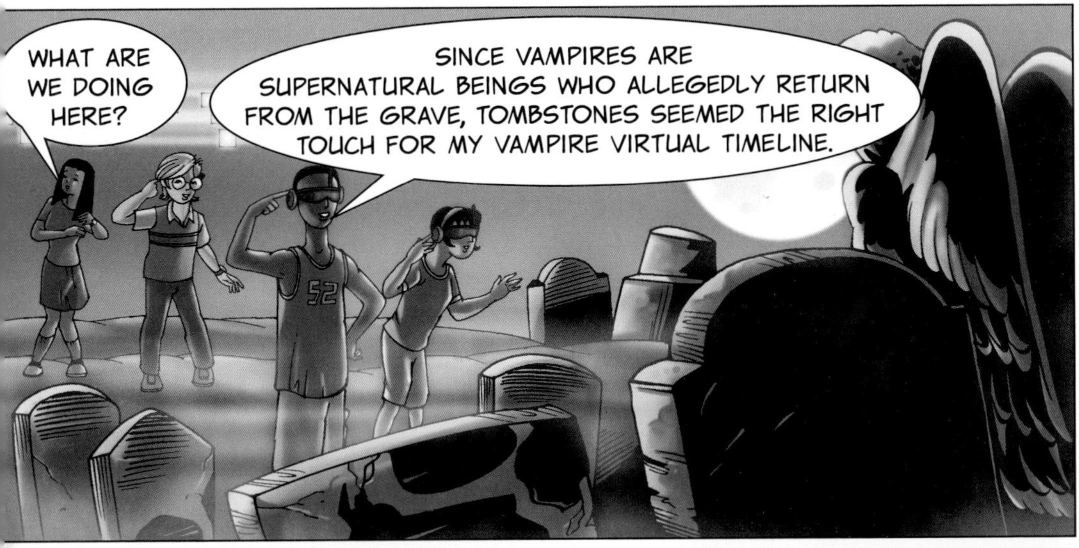
WHAT ARE WE DOING HERE?
SINCE VAMPIRES ARE SUPERNATURAL BEINGS WHO ALLEGEDLY RETURN FROM THE GRAVE, TOMBSTONES SEEMED THE RIGHT TOUCH FOR MY VAMPIRE VIRTUAL TIMELINE.

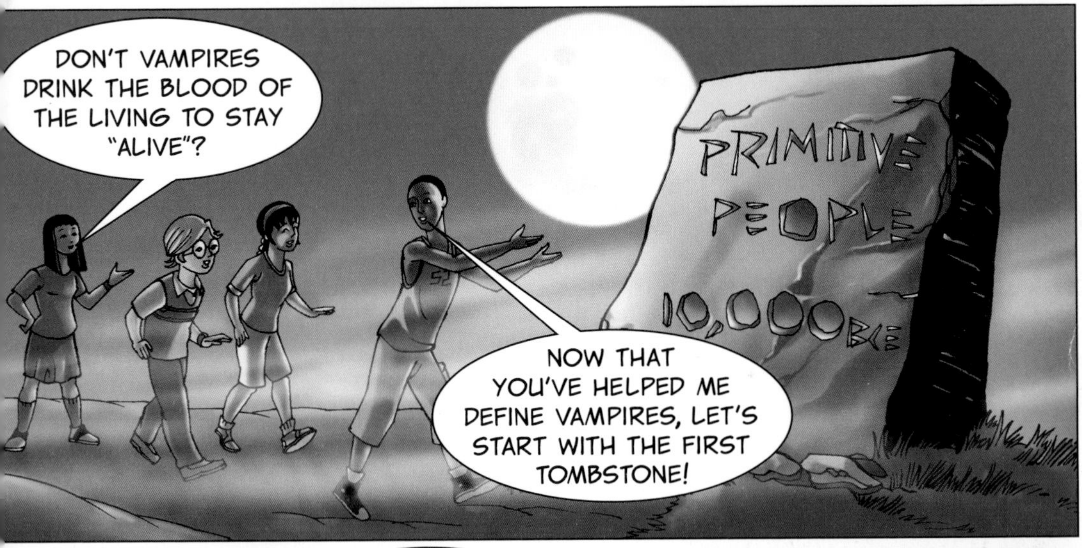
DON'T VAMPIRES DRINK THE BLOOD OF THE LIVING TO STAY "ALIVE"?
PRIMITIVE PEOPLE 10,000 BCE
NOW THAT YOU'VE HELPED ME DEFINE VAMPIRES, LET'S START WITH THE FIRST TOMBSTONE!

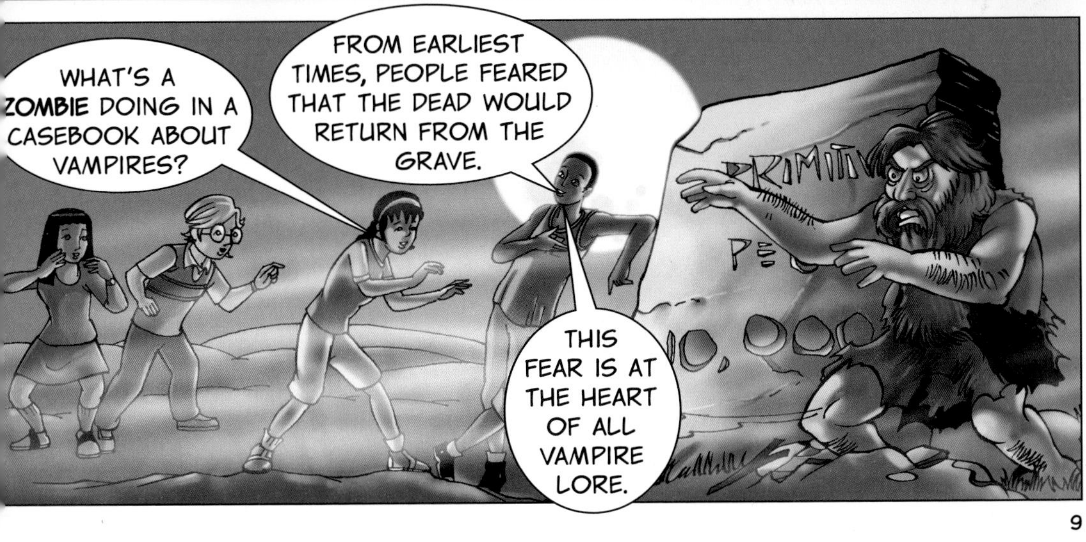
WHAT'S A ZOMBIE DOING IN A CASEBOOK ABOUT VAMPIRES?
FROM EARLIEST TIMES, PEOPLE FEARED THAT THE DEAD WOULD RETURN FROM THE GRAVE.
THIS FEAR IS AT THE HEART OF ALL VAMPIRE LORE.

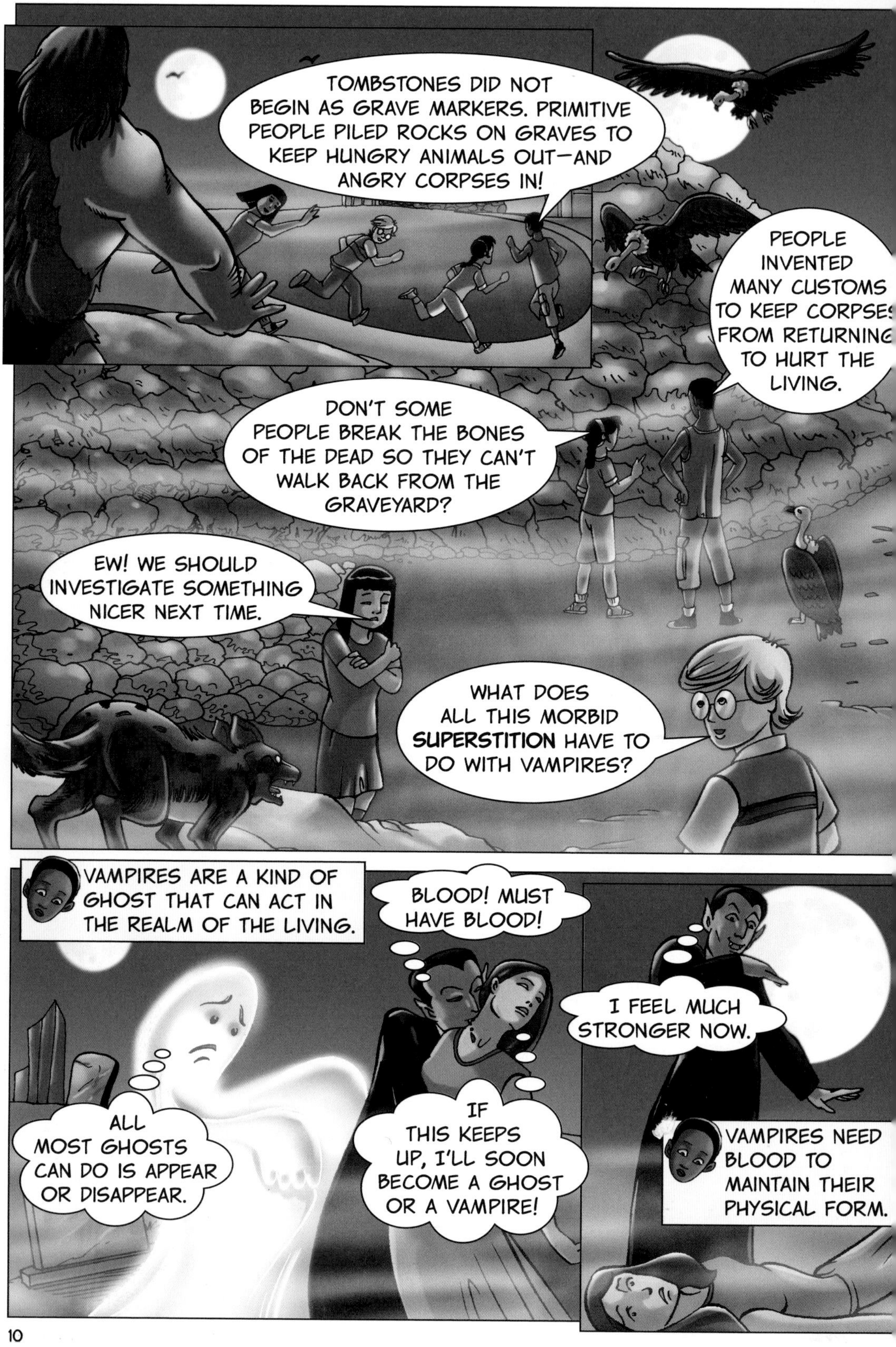
TOMBSTONES DID NOT BEGIN AS GRAVE MARKERS. PRIMITIVE PEOPLE PILED ROCKS ON GRAVES TO KEEP HUNGRY ANIMALS OUT—AND ANGRY CORPSES IN!
PEOPLE INVENTED MANY CUSTOMS TO KEEP CORPSES FROM RETURNING TO HURT THE LIVING.
DON'T SOME PEOPLE BREAK THE BONES OF THE DEAD SO THEY CAN'T WALK BACK FROM THE GRAVEYARD?
EW! WE SHOULD INVESTIGATE SOMETHING NICER NEXT TIME.
WHAT DOES ALL THIS MORBID **SUPERSTITION** HAVE TO DO WITH VAMPIRES?
VAMPIRES ARE A KIND OF GHOST THAT CAN ACT IN THE REALM OF THE LIVING.
BLOOD! MUST HAVE BLOOD!
ALL MOST GHOSTS CAN DO IS APPEAR OR DISAPPEAR.
IF THIS KEEPS UP, I'LL SOON BECOME A GHOST OR A VAMPIRE!
I FEEL MUCH STRONGER NOW.
VAMPIRES NEED BLOOD TO MAINTAIN THEIR PHYSICAL FORM.

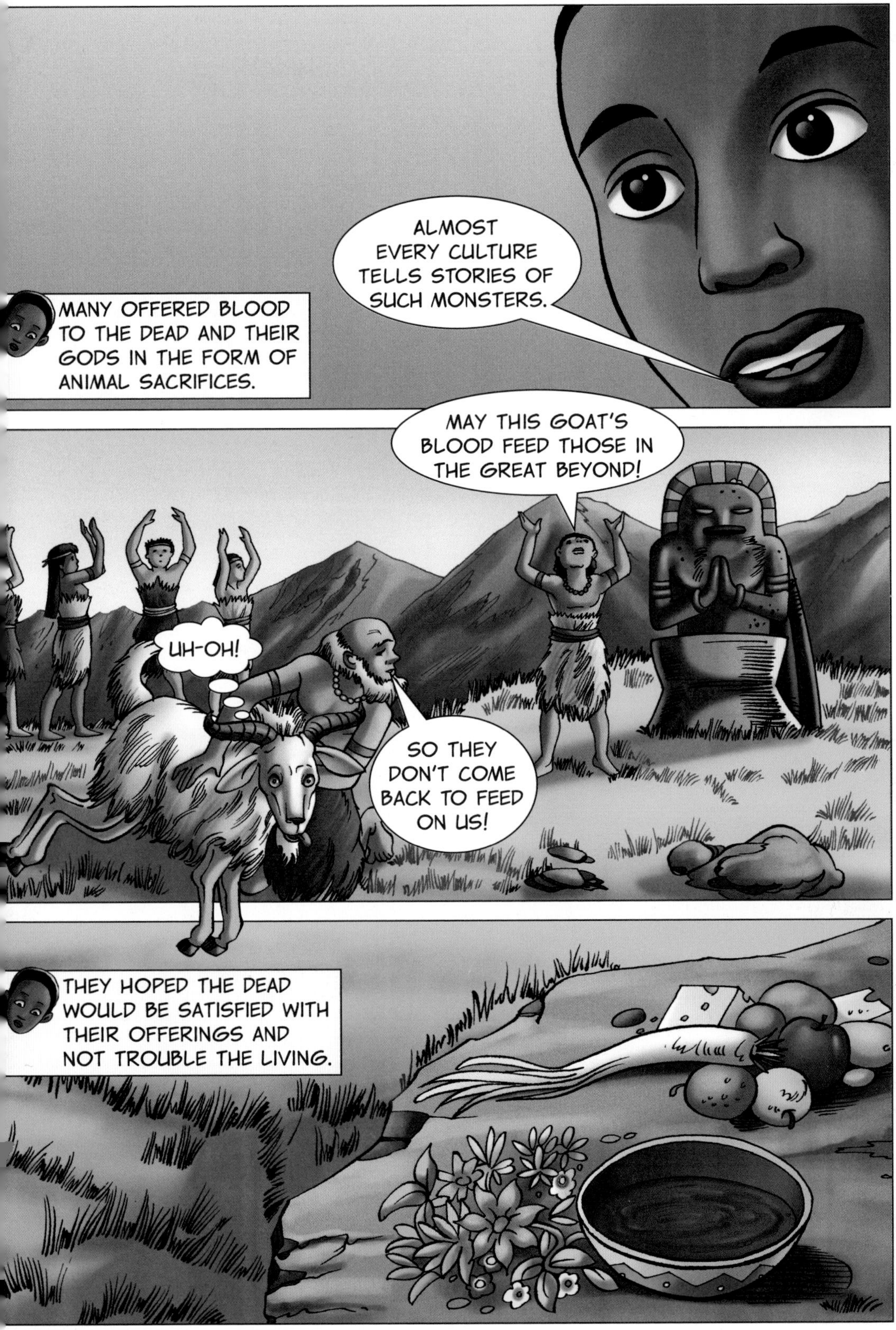
ALMOST EVERY CULTURE TELLS STORIES OF SUCH MONSTERS.
MANY OFFERED BLOOD TO THE DEAD AND THEIR GODS IN THE FORM OF ANIMAL SACRIFICES.
MAY THIS GOAT'S BLOOD FEED THOSE IN THE GREAT BEYOND!
UH-OH!
SO THEY DON'T COME BACK TO FEED ON US!
THEY HOPED THE DEAD WOULD BE SATISFIED WITH THEIR OFFERINGS AND NOT TROUBLE THE LIVING.

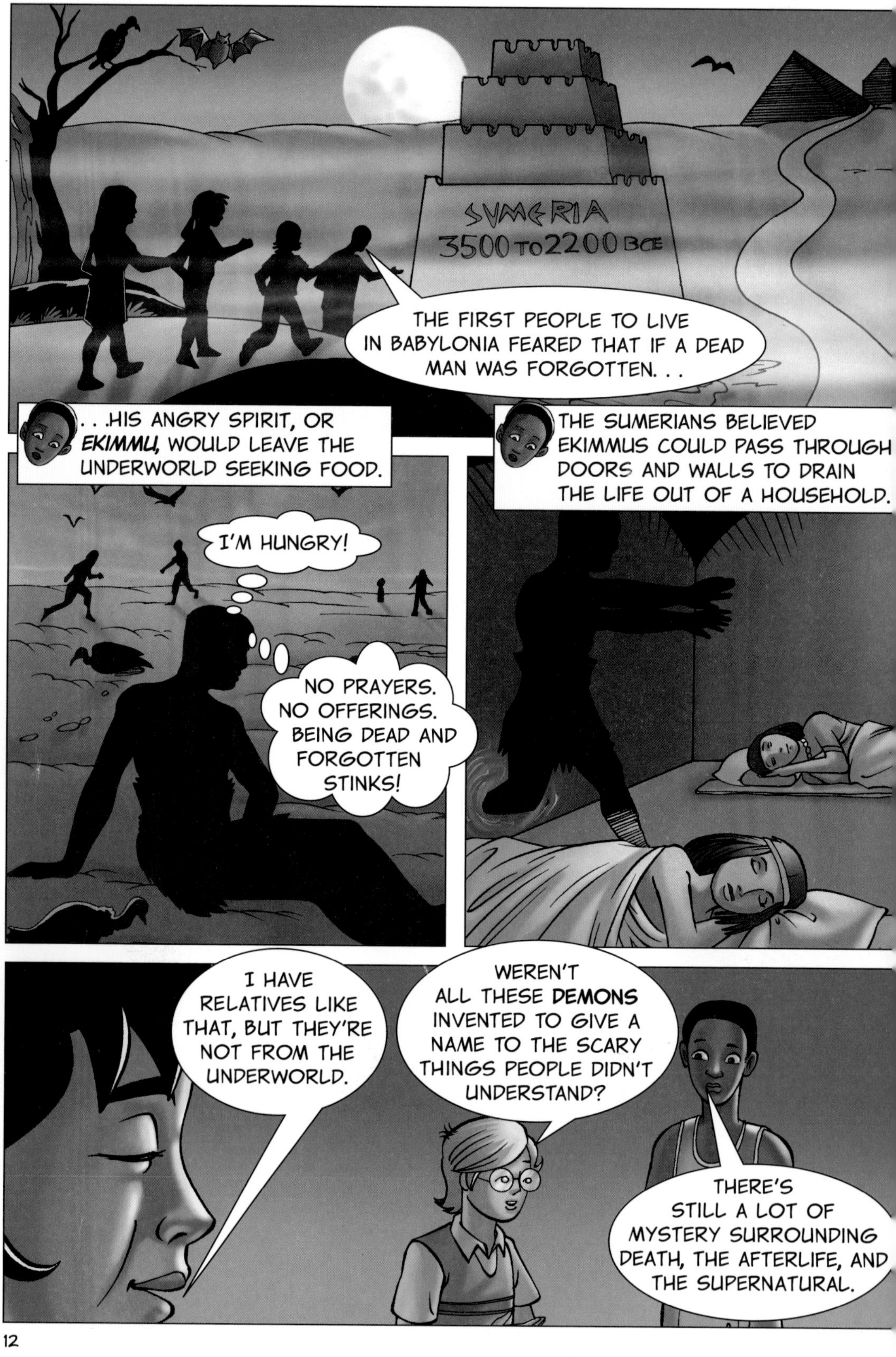
SUMERIA
3500 TO 2200 BCE
THE FIRST PEOPLE TO LIVE IN BABYLONIA FEARED THAT IF A DEAD MAN WAS FORGOTTEN. . .
. . .HIS ANGRY SPIRIT, OR **EKIMMU**, WOULD LEAVE THE UNDERWORLD SEEKING FOOD.
I'M HUNGRY!
NO PRAYERS. NO OFFERINGS. BEING DEAD AND FORGOTTEN STINKS!
THE SUMERIANS BELIEVED EKIMMUS COULD PASS THROUGH DOORS AND WALLS TO DRAIN THE LIFE OUT OF A HOUSEHOLD.
I HAVE RELATIVES LIKE THAT, BUT THEY'RE NOT FROM THE UNDERWORLD.
WEREN'T ALL THESE **DEMONS** INVENTED TO GIVE A NAME TO THE SCARY THINGS PEOPLE DIDN'T UNDERSTAND?
THERE'S STILL A LOT OF MYSTERY SURROUNDING DEATH, THE AFTERLIFE, AND THE SUPERNATURAL.

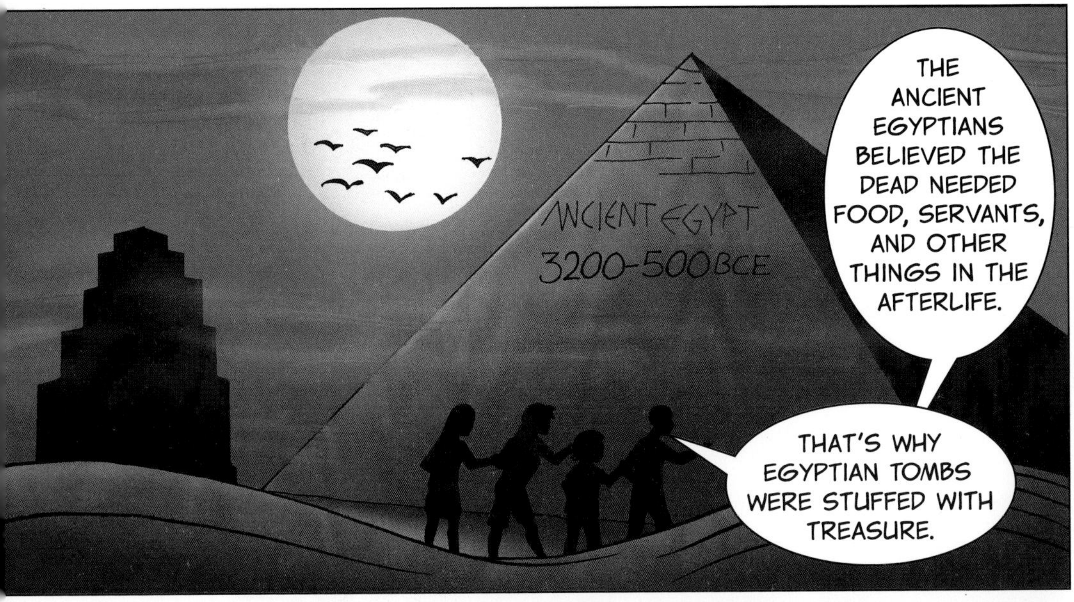
ANCIENT EGYPT
3200-500 BCE
THE ANCIENT EGYPTIANS BELIEVED THE DEAD NEEDED FOOD, SERVANTS, AND OTHER THINGS IN THE AFTERLIFE.
THAT'S WHY EGYPTIAN TOMBS WERE STUFFED WITH TREASURE.

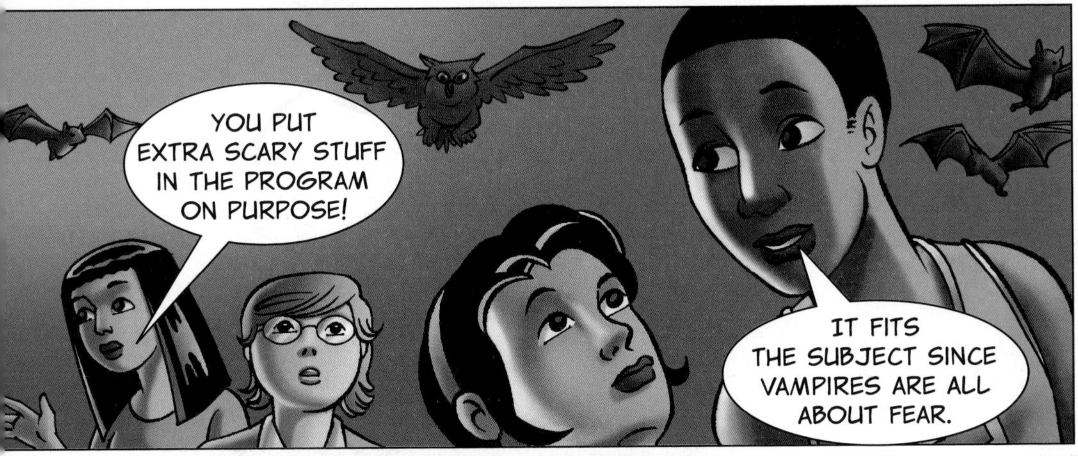
YOU PUT EXTRA SCARY STUFF IN THE PROGRAM ON PURPOSE!
IT FITS THE SUBJECT SINCE VAMPIRES ARE ALL ABOUT FEAR.

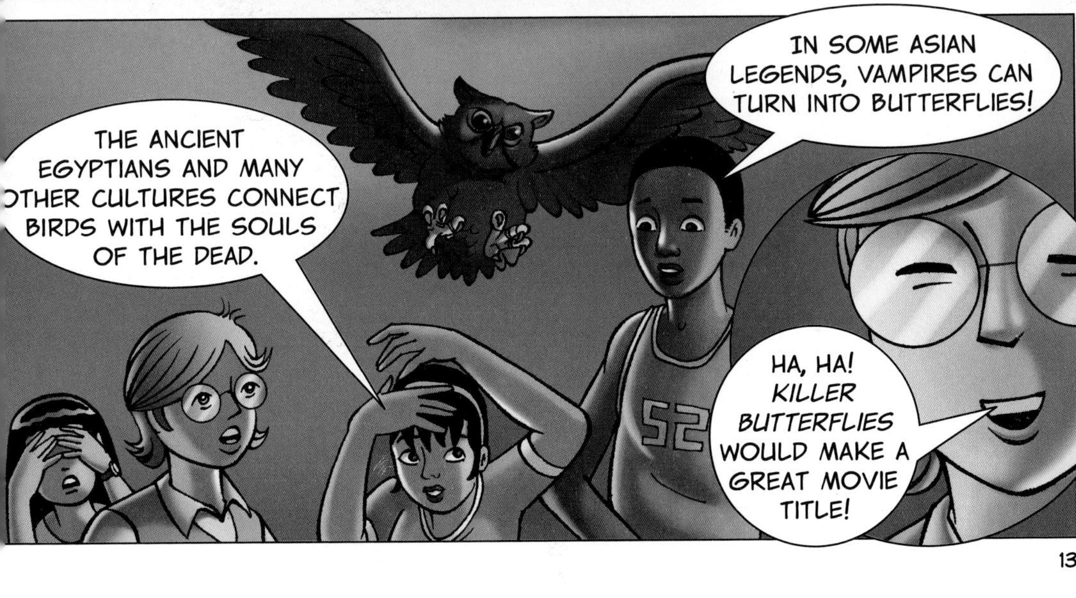
THE ANCIENT EGYPTIANS AND MANY OTHER CULTURES CONNECT BIRDS WITH THE SOULS OF THE DEAD.
IN SOME ASIAN LEGENDS, VAMPIRES CAN TURN INTO BUTTERFLIES!
HA, HA! KILLER BUTTERFLIES WOULD MAKE A GREAT MOVIE TITLE!
52

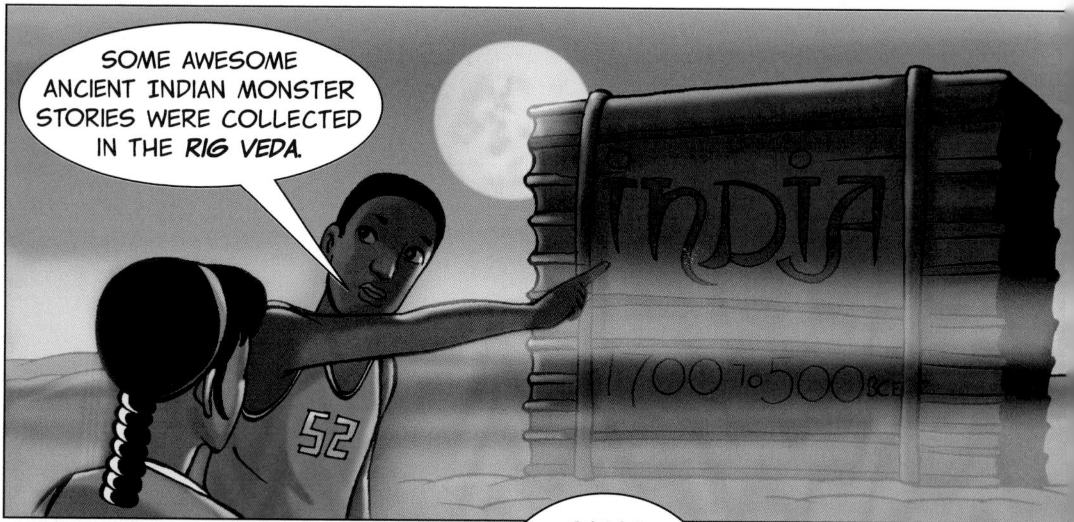
SOME AWESOME ANCIENT INDIAN MONSTER STORIES WERE COLLECTED IN THE RIG VEDA.
INDIA
1700 to 500 BCE

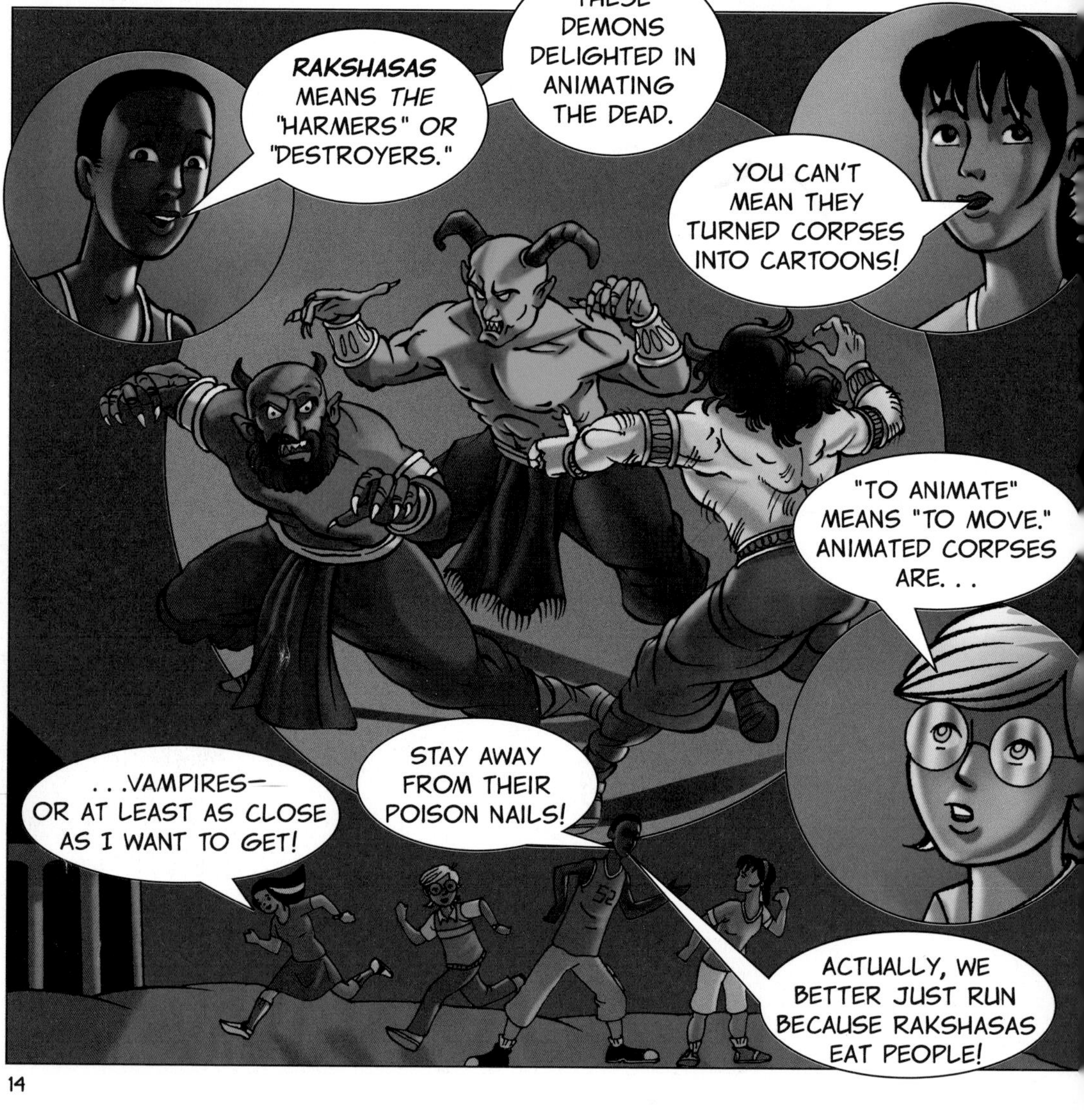
RAKSHASAS MEANS THE "HARMERS" OR "DESTROYERS."
THESE DEMONS DELIGHTED IN ANIMATING THE DEAD.
YOU CAN'T MEAN THEY TURNED CORPSES INTO CARTOONS!
"TO ANIMATE" MEANS "TO MOVE." ANIMATED CORPSES ARE. . .
. . .VAMPIRES— OR AT LEAST AS CLOSE AS I WANT TO GET!
STAY AWAY FROM THEIR POISON NAILS!
ACTUALLY, WE BETTER JUST RUN BECAUSE RAKSHASAS EAT PEOPLE!

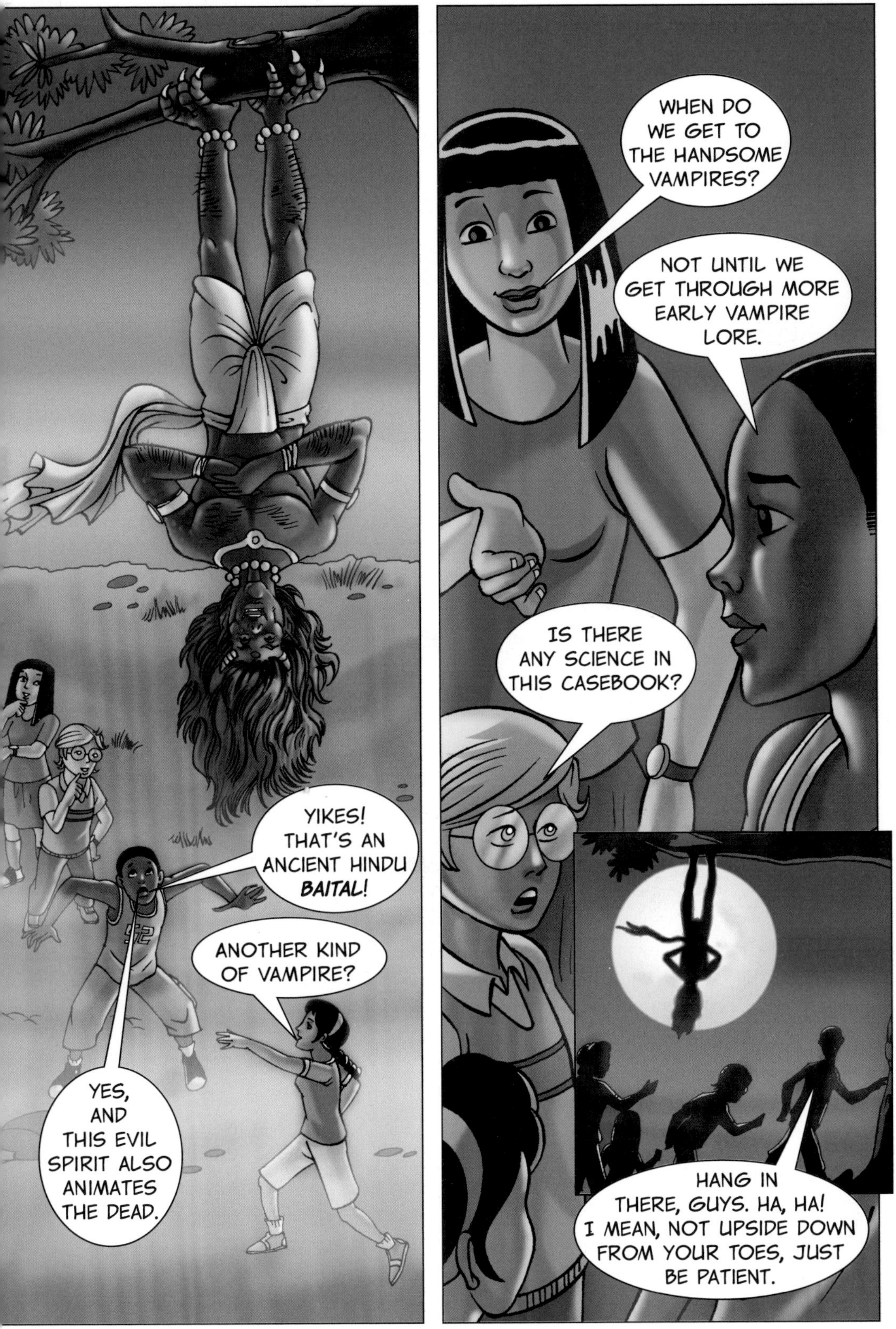
YIKES! THAT'S AN ANCIENT HINDU *BAITAL*!
ANOTHER KIND OF VAMPIRE?
YES, AND THIS EVIL SPIRIT ALSO ANIMATES THE DEAD.
WHEN DO WE GET TO THE HANDSOME VAMPIRES?
NOT UNTIL WE GET THROUGH MORE EARLY VAMPIRE LORE.
IS THERE ANY SCIENCE IN THIS CASEBOOK?
HANG IN THERE, GUYS. HA, HA! I MEAN, NOT UPSIDE DOWN FROM YOUR TOES, JUST BE PATIENT.

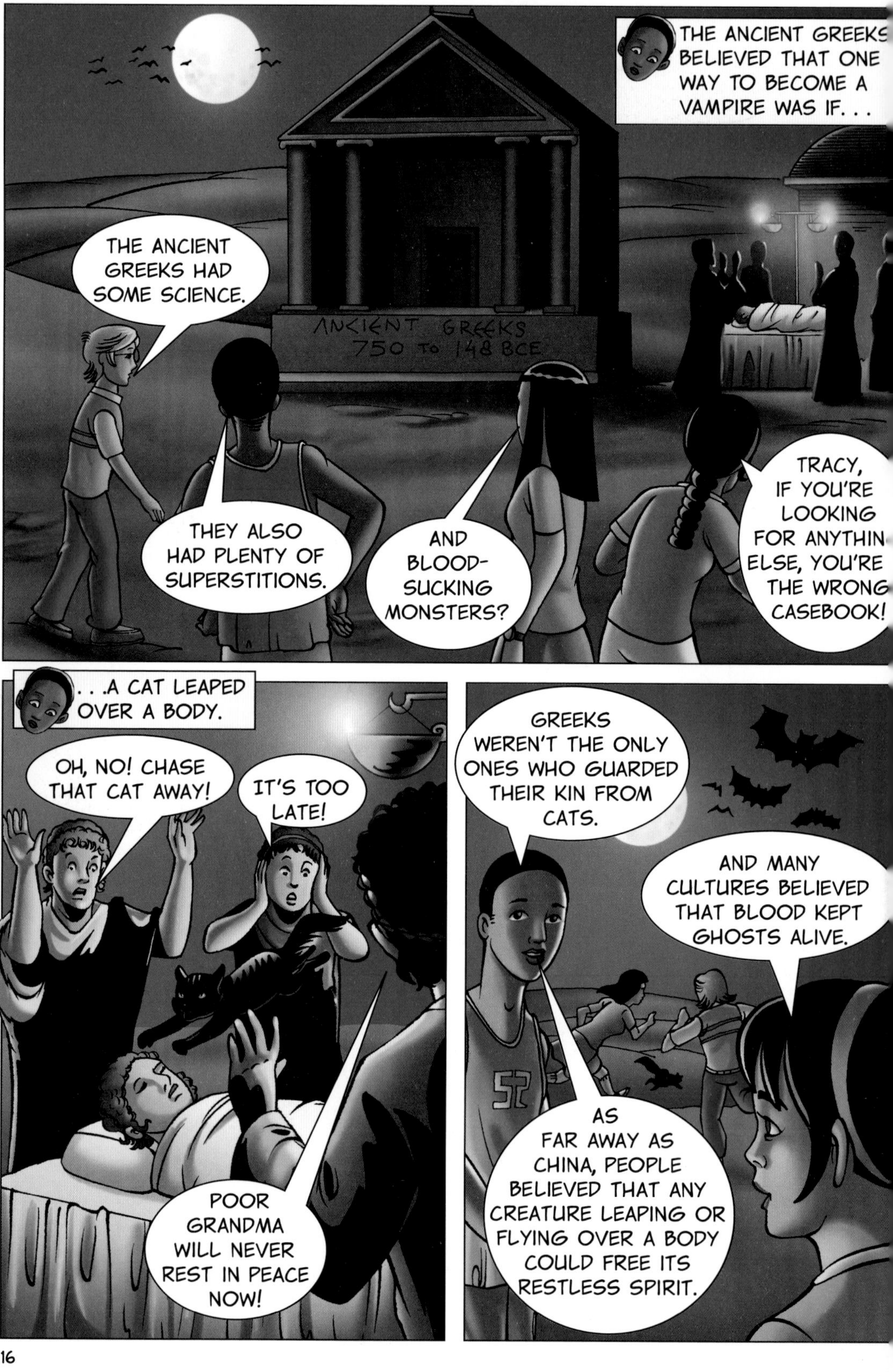

THE ANCIENT GREEKS BELIEVED THAT ONE WAY TO BECOME A VAMPIRE WAS IF. . .
ANCIENT GREEKS 750 TO 148 BCE
THE ANCIENT GREEKS HAD SOME SCIENCE.
THEY ALSO HAD PLENTY OF SUPERSTITIONS.
AND BLOOD-SUCKING MONSTERS?
TRACY, IF YOU'RE LOOKING FOR ANYTHIN ELSE, YOU'RE THE WRONG CASEBOOK!
. . .A CAT LEAPED OVER A BODY.
OH, NO! CHASE THAT CAT AWAY!
IT'S TOO LATE!
POOR GRANDMA WILL NEVER REST IN PEACE NOW!
GREEKS WEREN'T THE ONLY ONES WHO GUARDED THEIR KIN FROM CATS.
AND MANY CULTURES BELIEVED THAT BLOOD KEPT GHOSTS ALIVE.
AS FAR AWAY AS CHINA, PEOPLE BELIEVED THAT ANY CREATURE LEAPING OR FLYING OVER A BODY COULD FREE ITS RESTLESS SPIRIT.

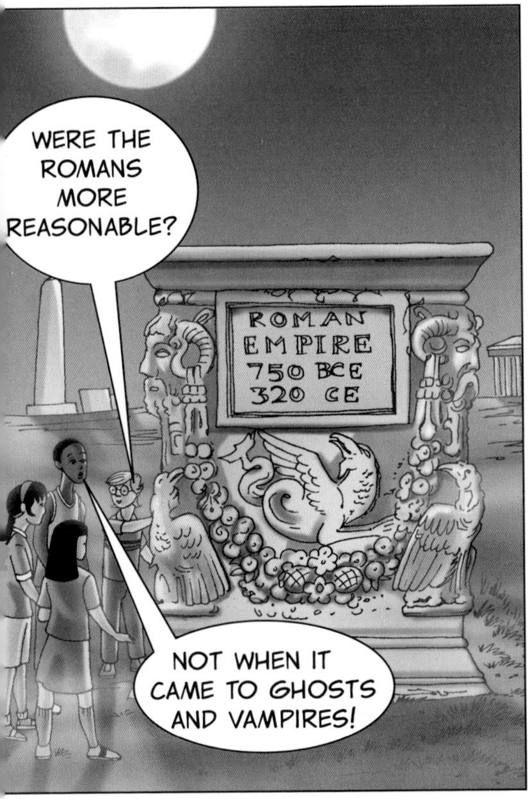
WERE THE ROMANS MORE REASONABLE?
ROMAN EMPIRE 750 BCE 320 CE
NOT WHEN IT CAME TO GHOSTS AND VAMPIRES!

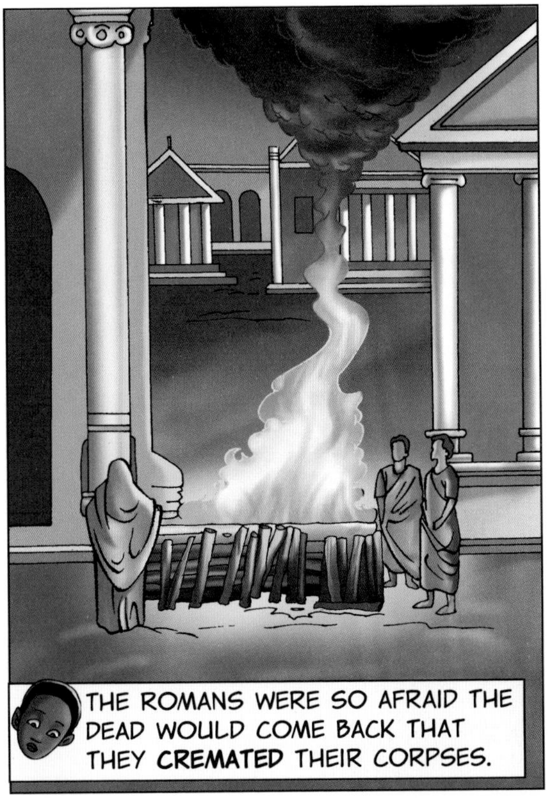
THE ROMANS WERE SO AFRAID THE DEAD WOULD COME BACK THAT THEY **CREMATED** THEIR CORPSES.

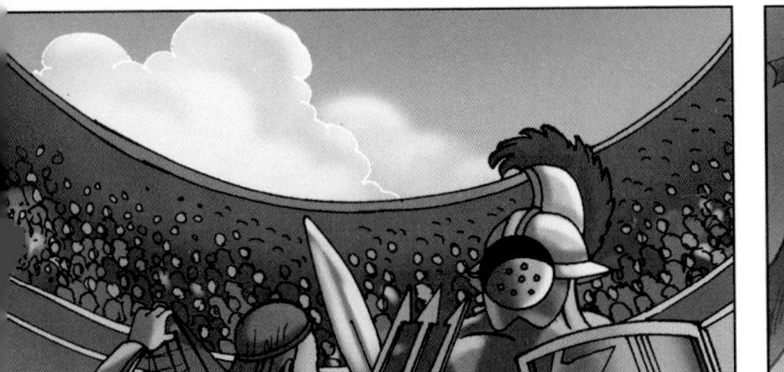
GLADIATOR BOUTS BEGAN AS FUNERAL GAMES. THE FIGHTERS' BLOOD FED THE SPIRIT OF THE HONORED DEAD.

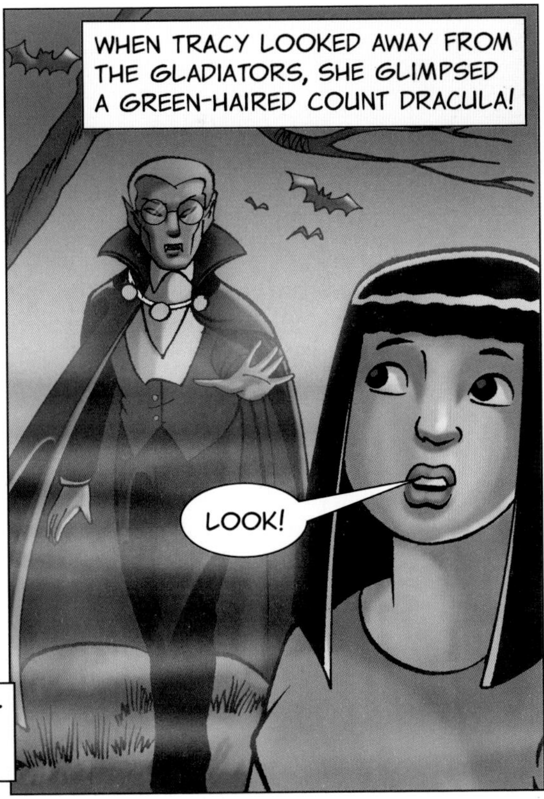
WHEN TRACY LOOKED AWAY FROM THE GLADIATORS, SHE GLIMPSED A GREEN-HAIRED COUNT DRACULA!
LOOK!

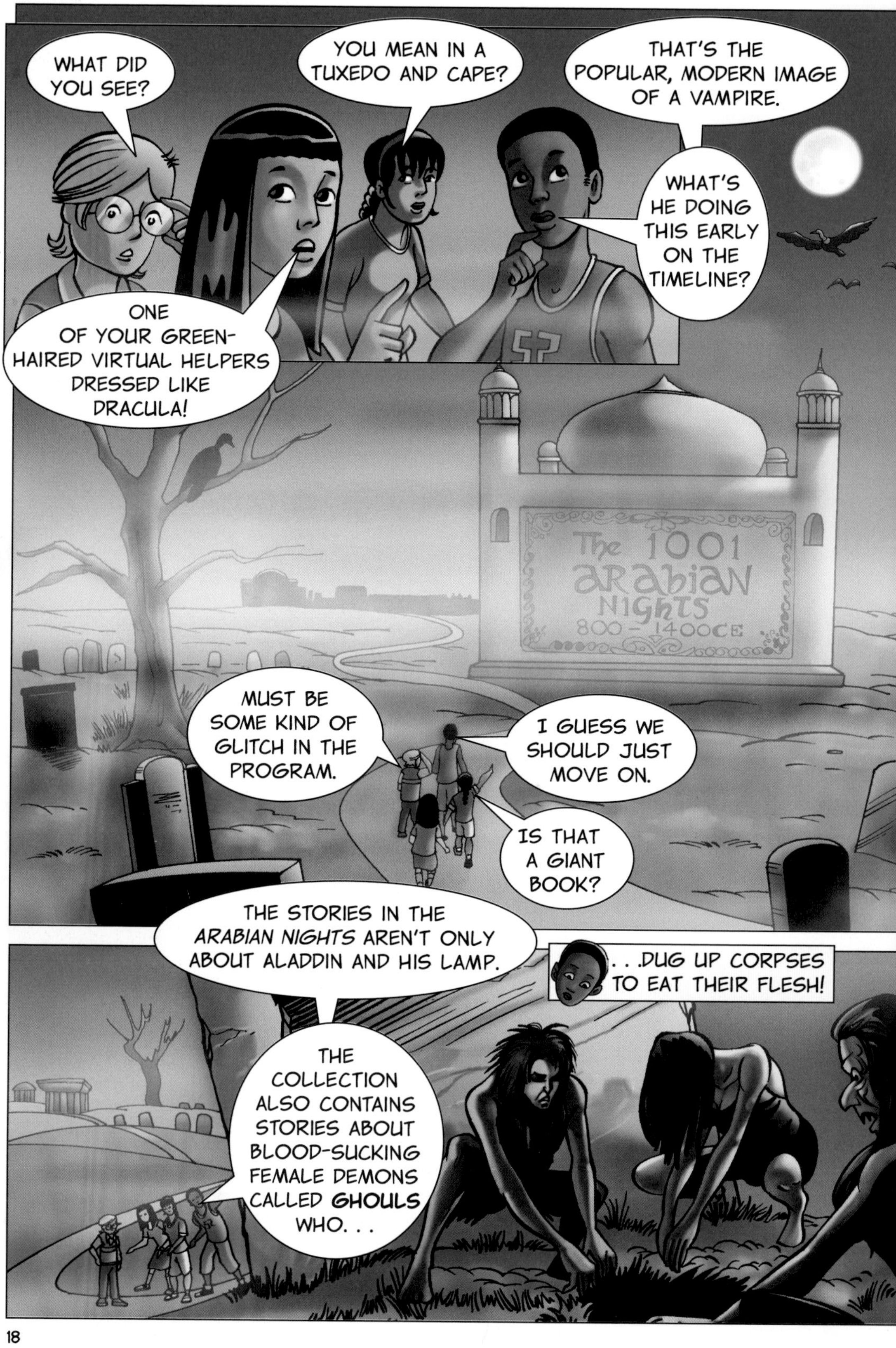
WHAT DID YOU SEE?
YOU MEAN IN A TUXEDO AND CAPE?
THAT'S THE POPULAR, MODERN IMAGE OF A VAMPIRE.
WHAT'S HE DOING THIS EARLY ON THE TIMELINE?
ONE OF YOUR GREEN-HAIRED VIRTUAL HELPERS DRESSED LIKE DRACULA!
The 1001 Arabian Nights 800 - 1400CE
MUST BE SOME KIND OF GLITCH IN THE PROGRAM.
I GUESS WE SHOULD JUST MOVE ON.
IS THAT A GIANT BOOK?
THE STORIES IN THE *ARABIAN NIGHTS* AREN'T ONLY ABOUT ALADDIN AND HIS LAMP.
THE COLLECTION ALSO CONTAINS STORIES ABOUT BLOOD-SUCKING FEMALE DEMONS CALLED **GHOULS** WHO. . .
. . .DUG UP CORPSES TO EAT THEIR FLESH!

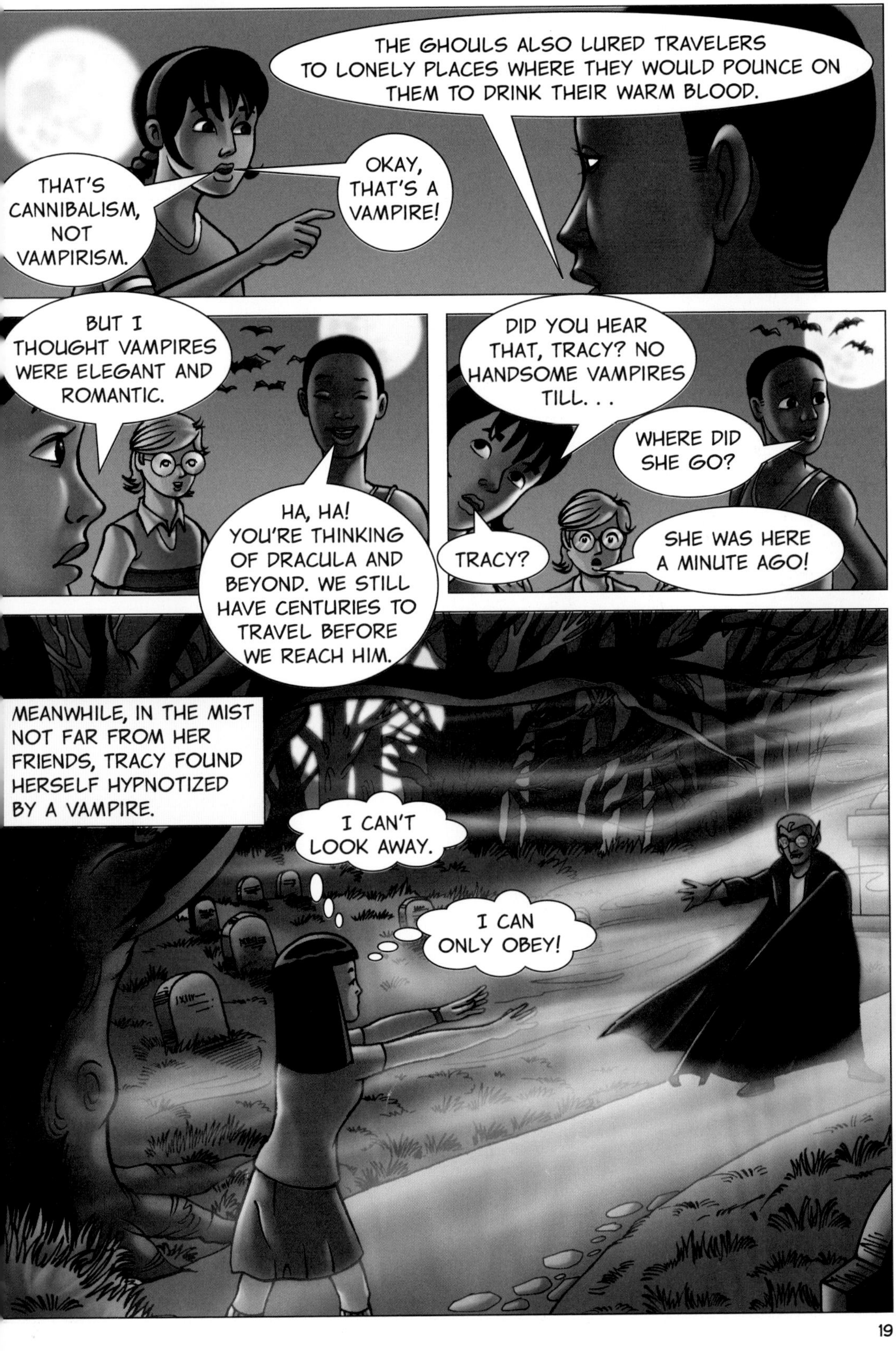
THE GHOULS ALSO LURED TRAVELERS TO LONELY PLACES WHERE THEY WOULD POUNCE ON THEM TO DRINK THEIR WARM BLOOD.
OKAY, THAT'S A VAMPIRE!
THAT'S CANNIBALISM, NOT VAMPIRISM.
BUT I THOUGHT VAMPIRES WERE ELEGANT AND ROMANTIC.
HA, HA! YOU'RE THINKING OF DRACULA AND BEYOND. WE STILL HAVE CENTURIES TO TRAVEL BEFORE WE REACH HIM.
DID YOU HEAR THAT, TRACY? NO HANDSOME VAMPIRES TILL. . .
WHERE DID SHE GO?
TRACY?
SHE WAS HERE A MINUTE AGO!
MEANWHILE, IN THE MIST NOT FAR FROM HER FRIENDS, TRACY FOUND HERSELF HYPNOTIZED BY A VAMPIRE.
I CAN'T LOOK AWAY.
I CAN ONLY OBEY!

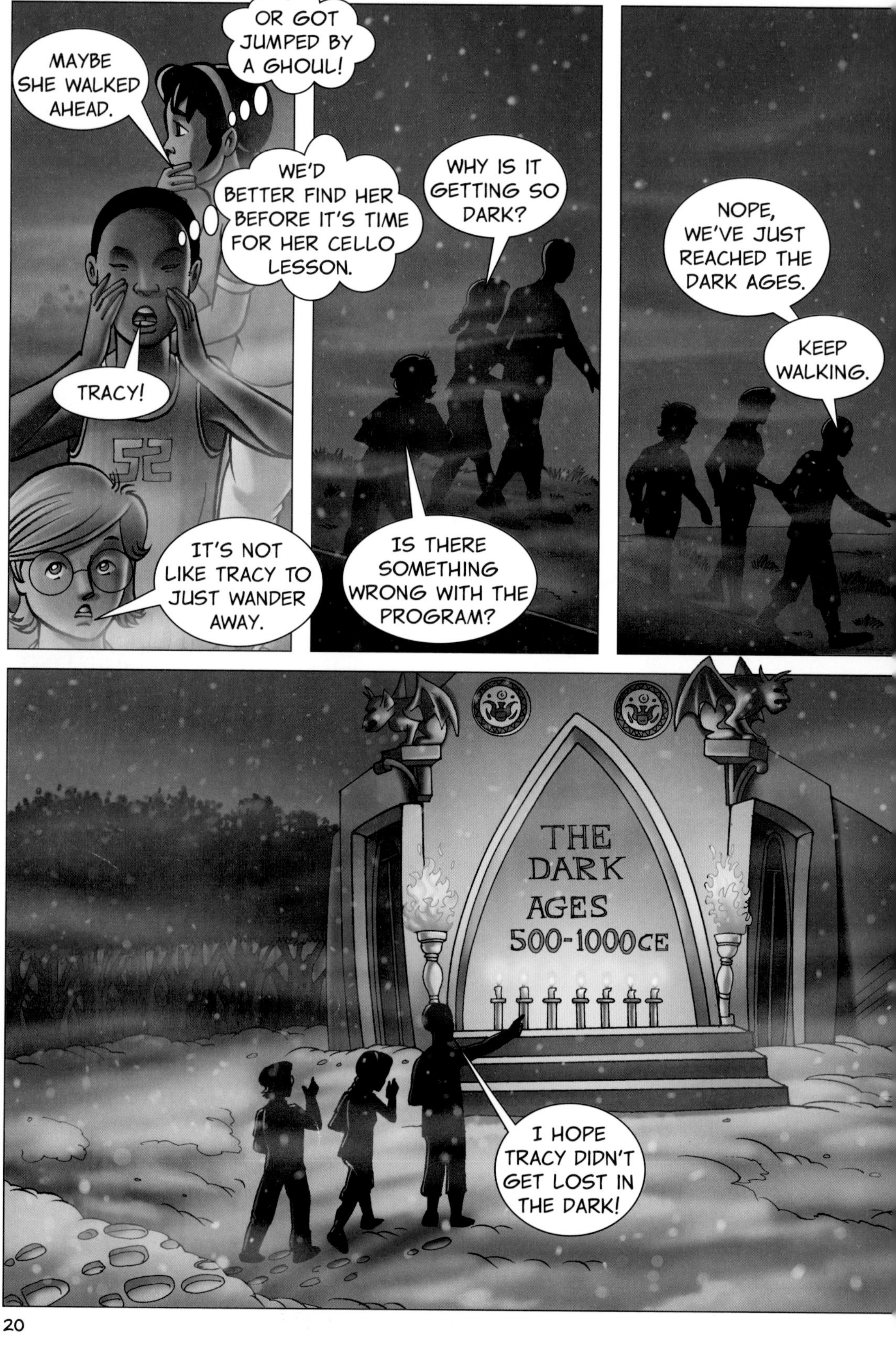
MAYBE SHE WALKED AHEAD.
OR GOT JUMPED BY A GHOUL!
WE'D BETTER FIND HER BEFORE IT'S TIME FOR HER CELLO LESSON.
TRACY!
IT'S NOT LIKE TRACY TO JUST WANDER AWAY.
WHY IS IT GETTING SO DARK?
IS THERE SOMETHING WRONG WITH THE PROGRAM?
NOPE, WE'VE JUST REACHED THE DARK AGES.
KEEP WALKING.
THE DARK AGES 500-1000CE
I HOPE TRACY DIDN'T GET LOST IN THE DARK!

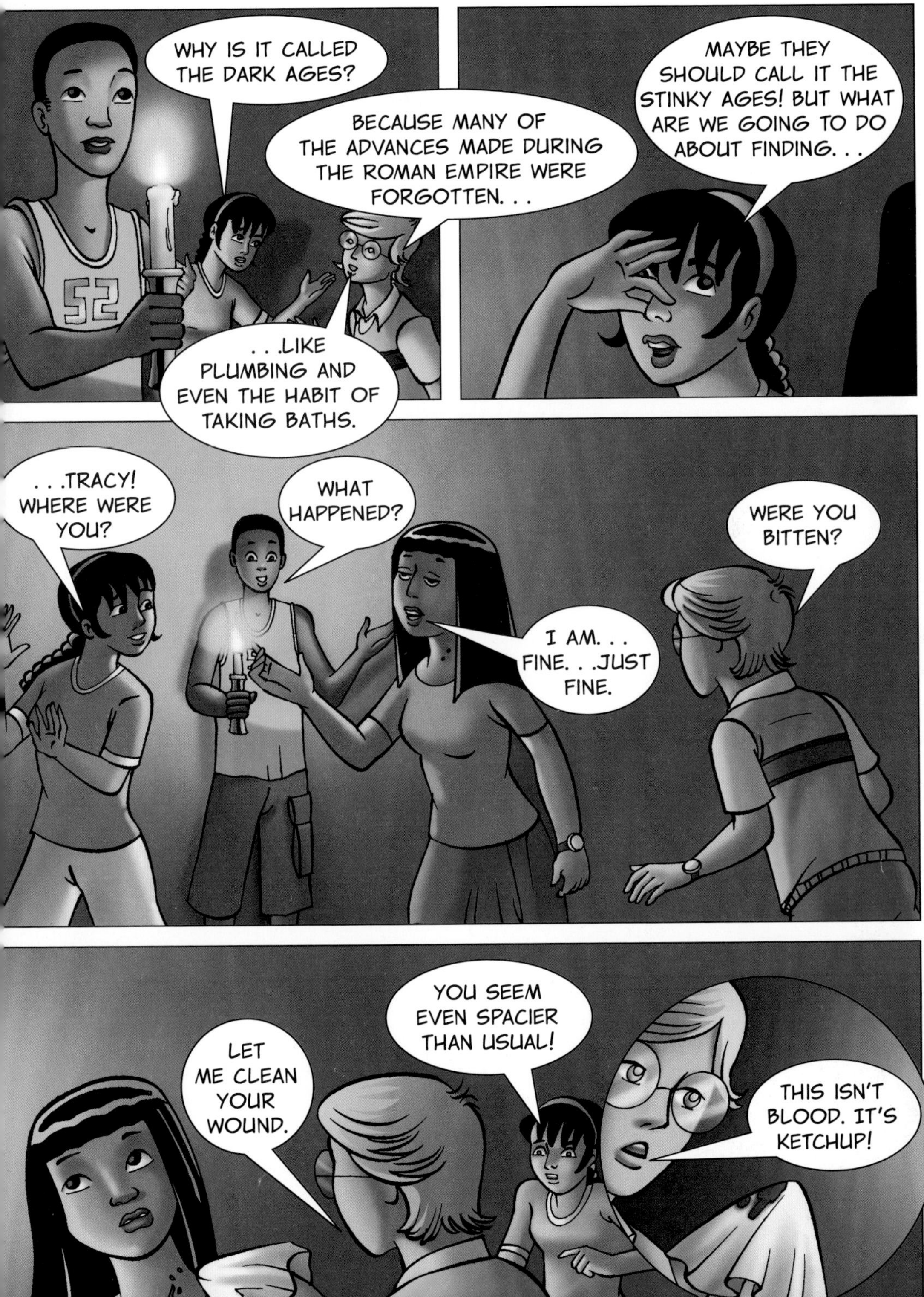
WHY IS IT CALLED THE DARK AGES?
BECAUSE MANY OF THE ADVANCES MADE DURING THE ROMAN EMPIRE WERE FORGOTTEN. . .
. . .LIKE PLUMBING AND EVEN THE HABIT OF TAKING BATHS.
MAYBE THEY SHOULD CALL IT THE STINKY AGES! BUT WHAT ARE WE GOING TO DO ABOUT FINDING. . .
. . .TRACY! WHERE WERE YOU?
WHAT HAPPENED?
I AM. . . FINE. . .JUST FINE.
WERE YOU BITTEN?
LET ME CLEAN YOUR WOUND.
YOU SEEM EVEN SPACIER THAN USUAL!
THIS ISN'T BLOOD. IT'S KETCHUP!

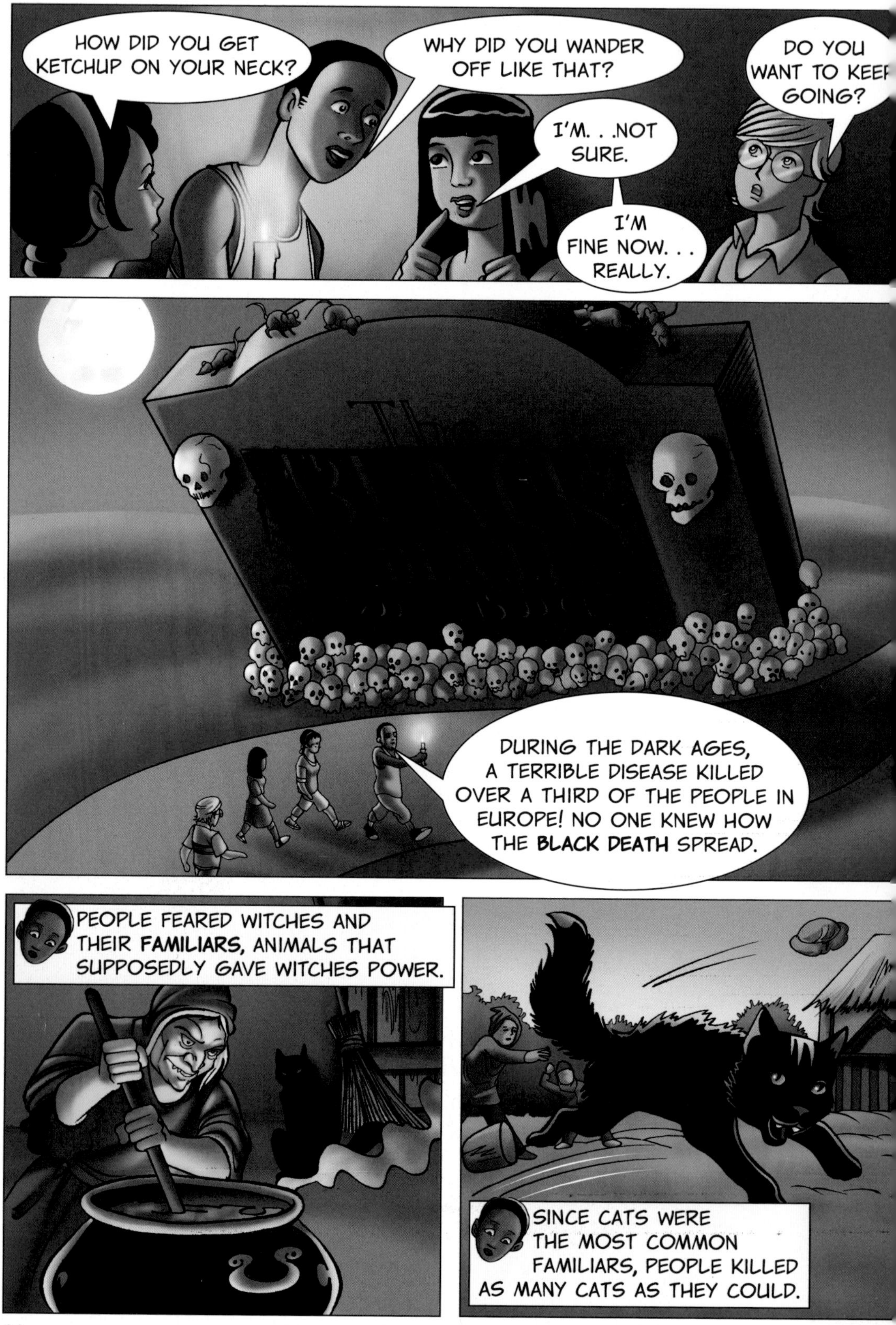
HOW DID YOU GET KETCHUP ON YOUR NECK?
WHY DID YOU WANDER OFF LIKE THAT?
DO YOU WANT TO KEEP GOING?
I'M. . .NOT SURE.
I'M FINE NOW. . . REALLY.
DURING THE DARK AGES, A TERRIBLE DISEASE KILLED OVER A THIRD OF THE PEOPLE IN EUROPE! NO ONE KNEW HOW THE BLACK DEATH SPREAD.
PEOPLE FEARED WITCHES AND THEIR FAMILIARS, ANIMALS THAT SUPPOSEDLY GAVE WITCHES POWER.
SINCE CATS WERE THE MOST COMMON FAMILIARS, PEOPLE KILLED AS MANY CATS AS THEY COULD.

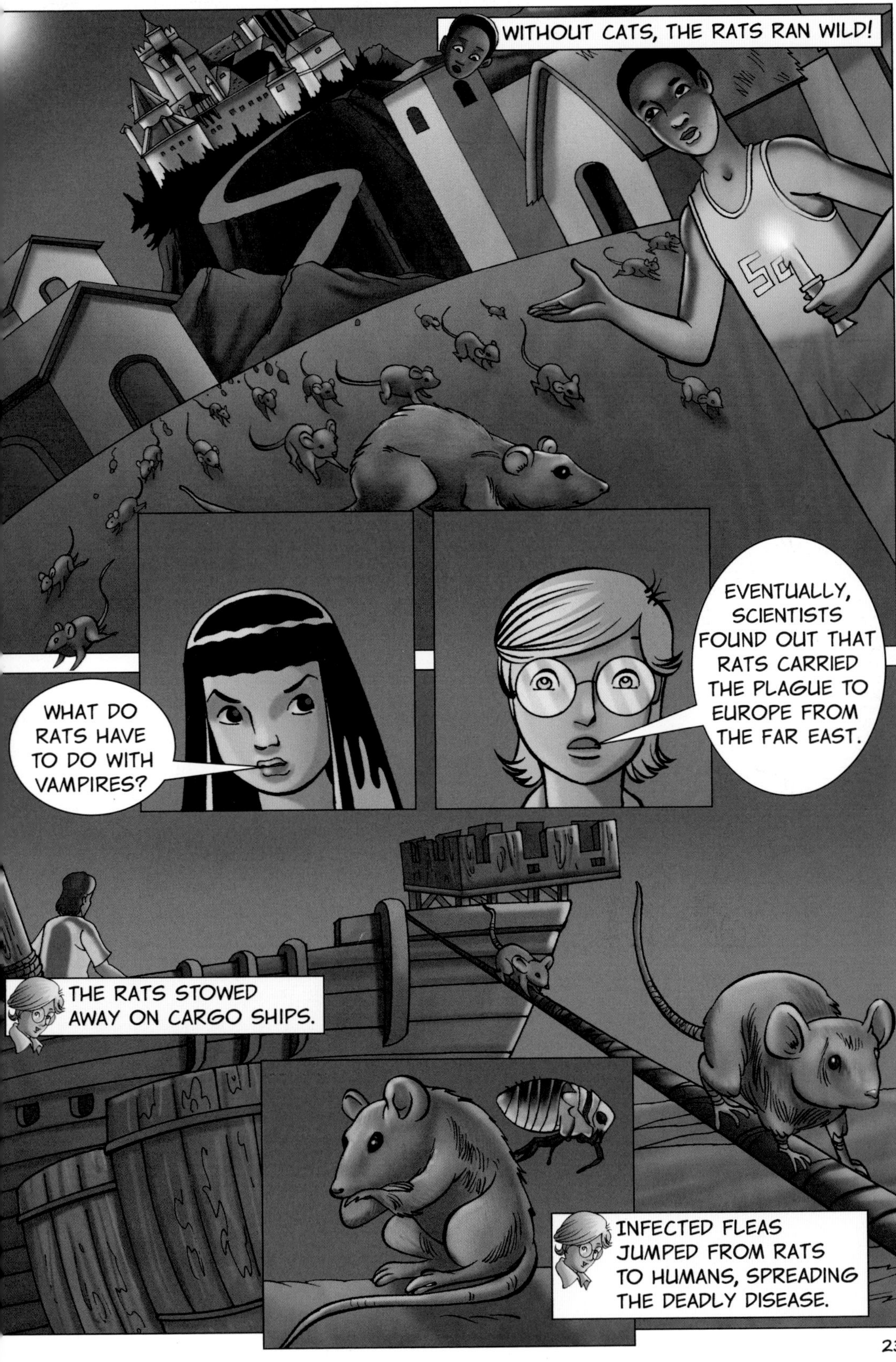
WITHOUT CATS, THE RATS RAN WILD!
WHAT DO RATS HAVE TO DO WITH VAMPIRES?
EVENTUALLY, SCIENTISTS FOUND OUT THAT RATS CARRIED THE PLAGUE TO EUROPE FROM THE FAR EAST.
THE RATS STOWED AWAY ON CARGO SHIPS.
INFECTED FLEAS JUMPED FROM RATS TO HUMANS, SPREADING THE DEADLY DISEASE.

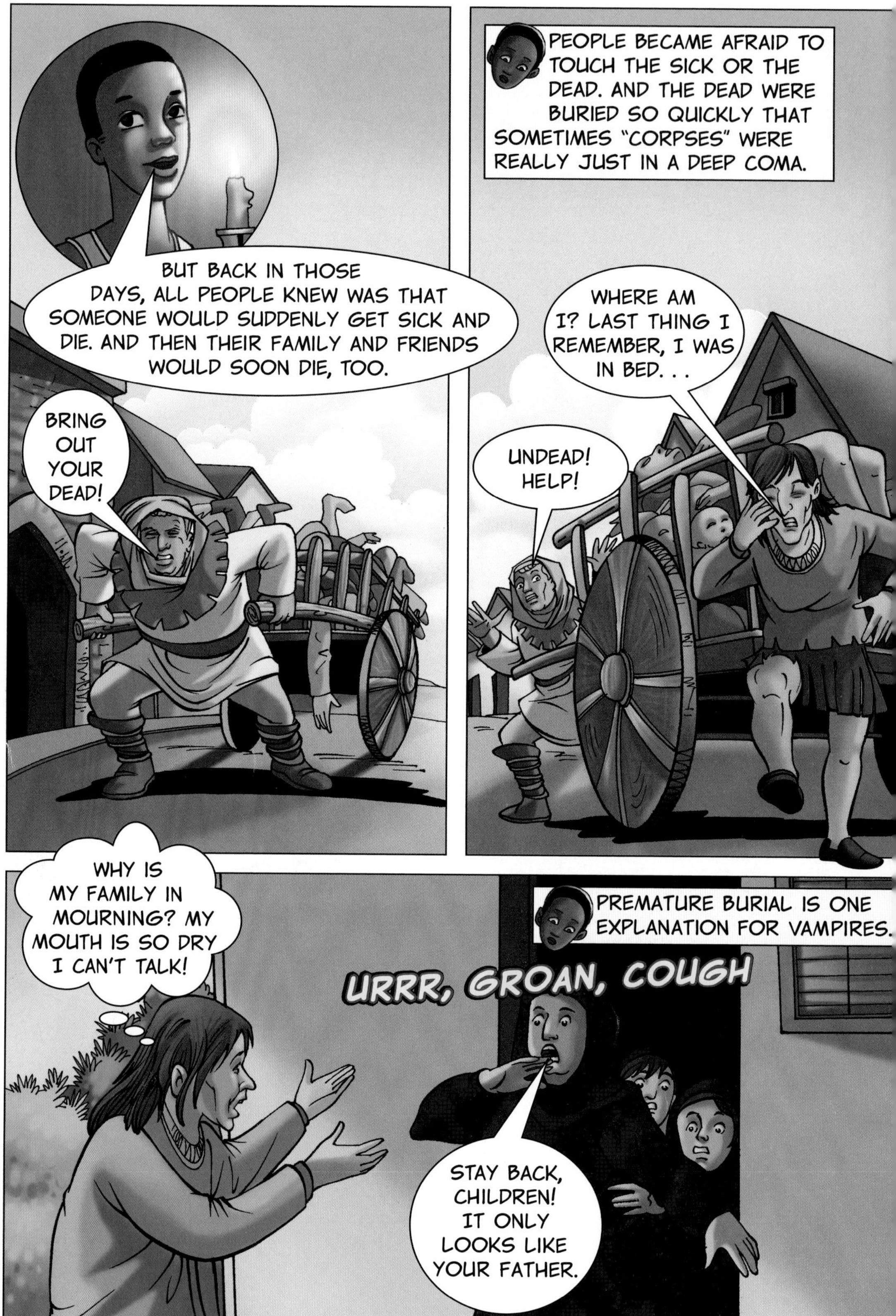
BUT BACK IN THOSE DAYS, ALL PEOPLE KNEW WAS THAT SOMEONE WOULD SUDDENLY GET SICK AND DIE. AND THEN THEIR FAMILY AND FRIENDS WOULD SOON DIE, TOO.
BRING OUT YOUR DEAD!
PEOPLE BECAME AFRAID TO TOUCH THE SICK OR THE DEAD. AND THE DEAD WERE BURIED SO QUICKLY THAT SOMETIMES "CORPSES" WERE REALLY JUST IN A DEEP COMA.
WHERE AM I? LAST THING I REMEMBER, I WAS IN BED. . .
UNDEAD! HELP!
WHY IS MY FAMILY IN MOURNING? MY MOUTH IS SO DRY I CAN'T TALK!
PREMATURE BURIAL IS ONE EXPLANATION FOR VAMPIRES.
URRR, GROAN, COUGH
STAY BACK, CHILDREN! IT ONLY LOOKS LIKE YOUR FATHER.

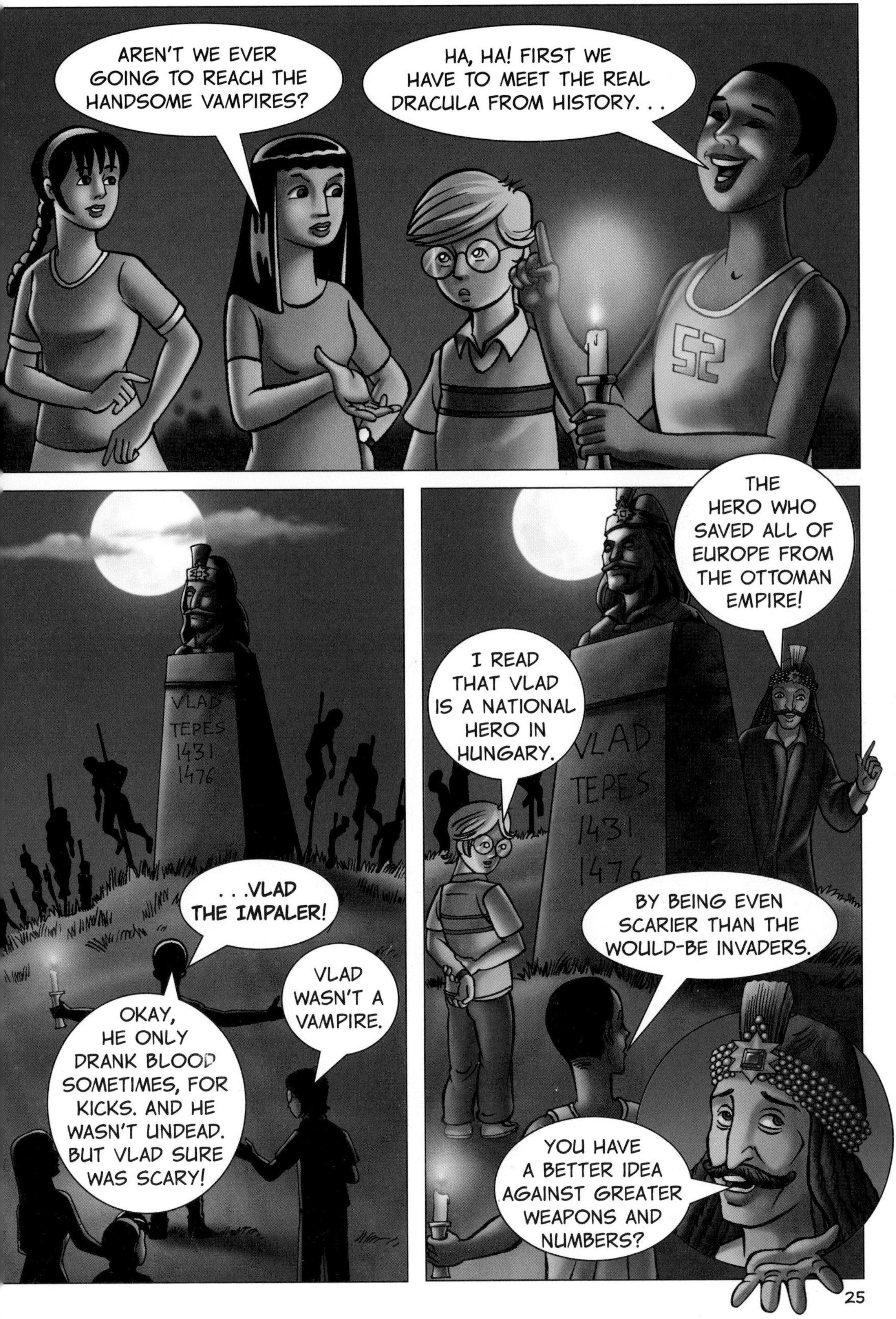
AREN'T WE EVER GOING TO REACH THE HANDSOME VAMPIRES?
HA, HA! FIRST WE HAVE TO MEET THE REAL DRACULA FROM HISTORY. . .
VLAD TEPES 1431 1476
. . .VLAD THE IMPALER!
OKAY, HE ONLY DRANK BLOOD SOMETIMES, FOR KICKS. AND HE WASN'T UNDEAD. BUT VLAD SURE WAS SCARY!
VLAD WASN'T A VAMPIRE.
THE HERO WHO SAVED ALL OF EUROPE FROM THE OTTOMAN EMPIRE!
I READ THAT VLAD IS A NATIONAL HERO IN HUNGARY.
VLAD TEPES 1431 1476
BY BEING EVEN SCARIER THAN THE WOULD-BE INVADERS.
YOU HAVE A BETTER IDEA AGAINST GREATER WEAPONS AND NUMBERS?

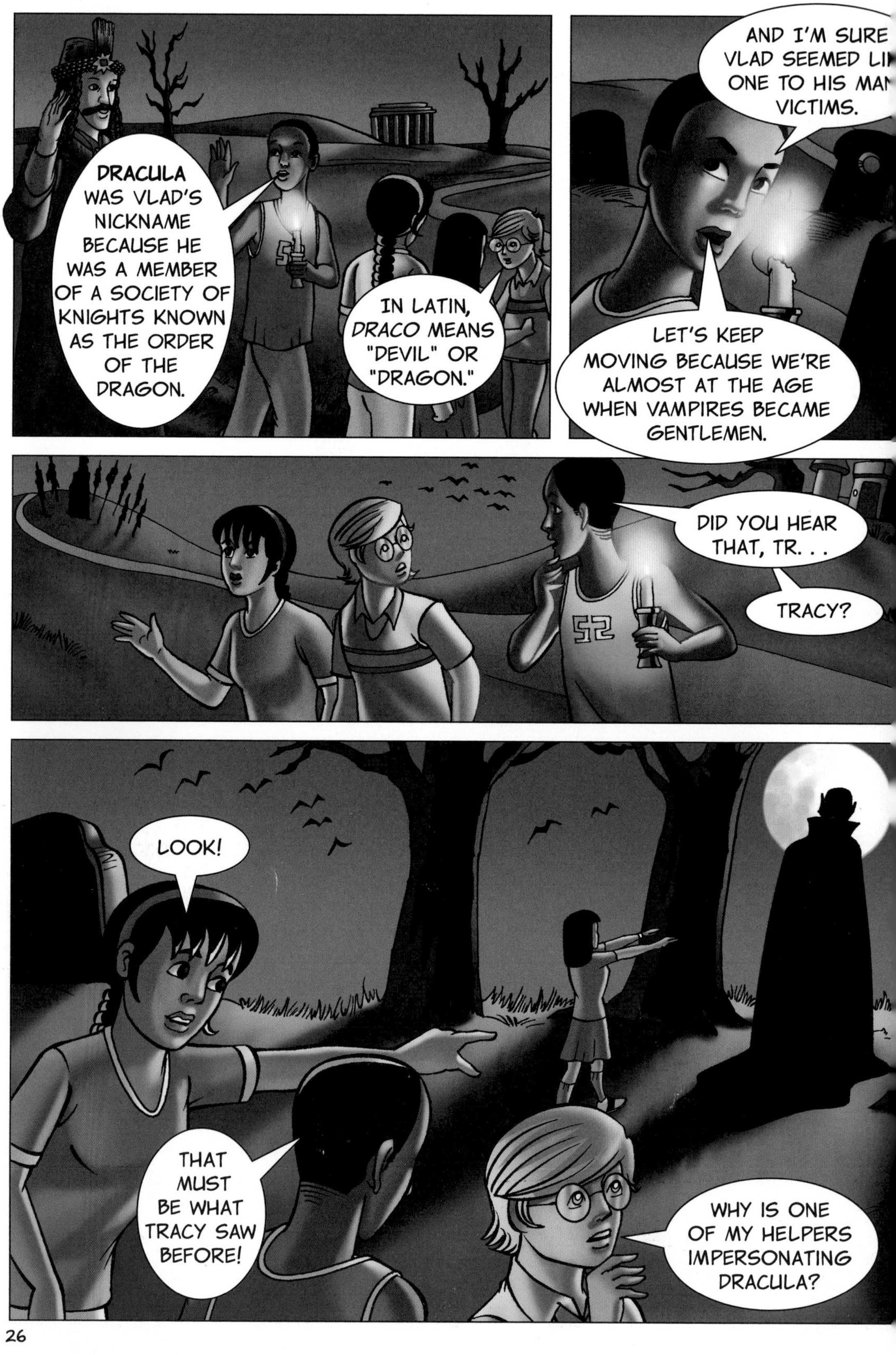
DRACULA WAS VLAD'S NICKNAME BECAUSE HE WAS A MEMBER OF A SOCIETY OF KNIGHTS KNOWN AS THE ORDER OF THE DRAGON.
IN LATIN, DRACO MEANS "DEVIL" OR "DRAGON."
AND I'M SURE VLAD SEEMED LI
ONE TO HIS MA
VICTIMS.
LET'S KEEP MOVING BECAUSE WE'RE ALMOST AT THE AGE WHEN VAMPIRES BECAME GENTLEMEN.
DID YOU HEAR THAT, TR. . .
TRACY?
LOOK!
THAT MUST BE WHAT TRACY SAW BEFORE!
WHY IS ONE OF MY HELPERS IMPERSONATING DRACULA?

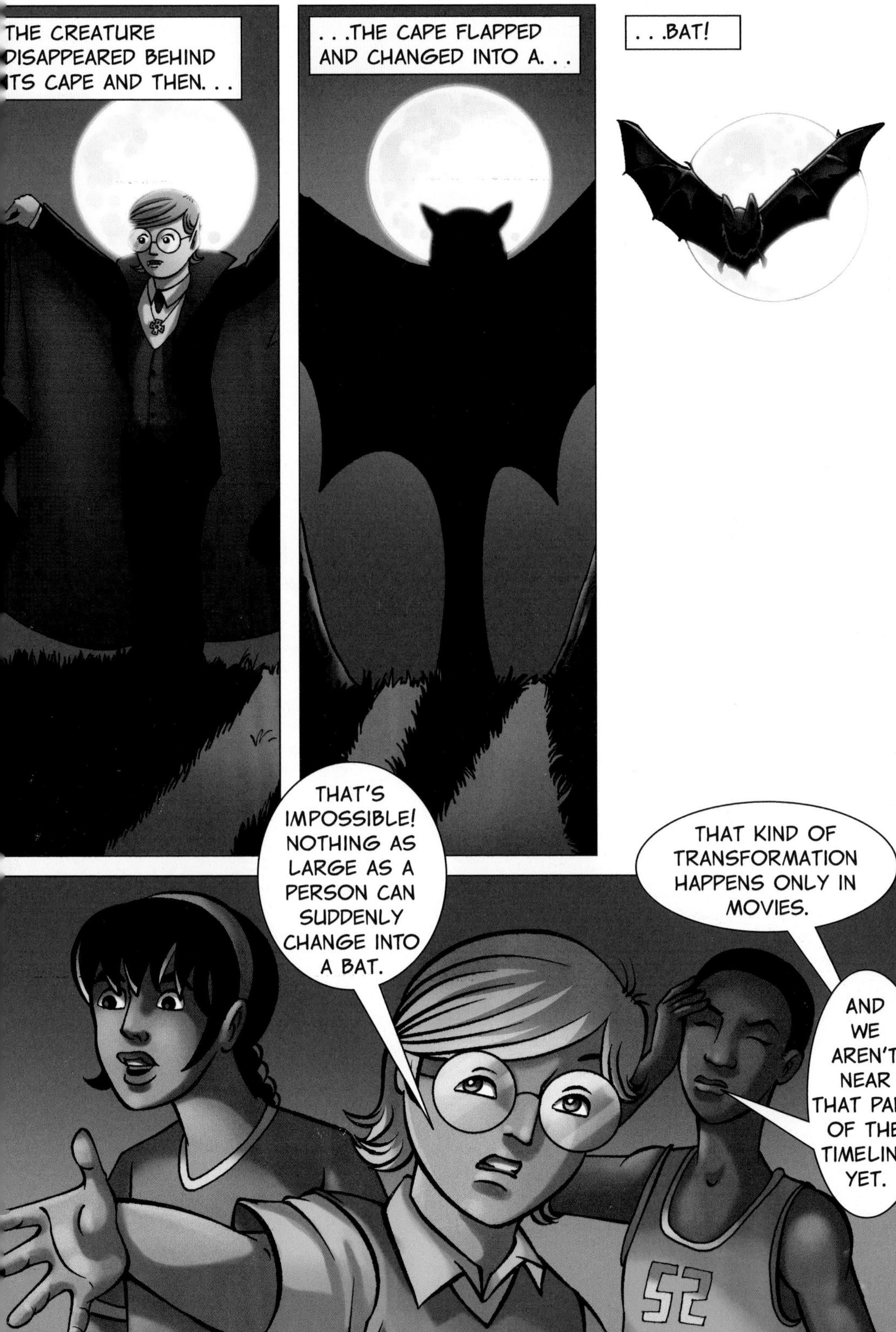
THE CREATURE DISAPPEARED BEHIND ITS CAPE AND THEN. . .
. . .THE CAPE FLAPPED AND CHANGED INTO A. . .
. . .BAT!
THAT'S IMPOSSIBLE! NOTHING AS LARGE AS A PERSON CAN SUDDENLY CHANGE INTO A BAT.
THAT KIND OF TRANSFORMATION HAPPENS ONLY IN MOVIES.
AND WE AREN'T NEAR THAT PART OF THE TIMELINE YET.

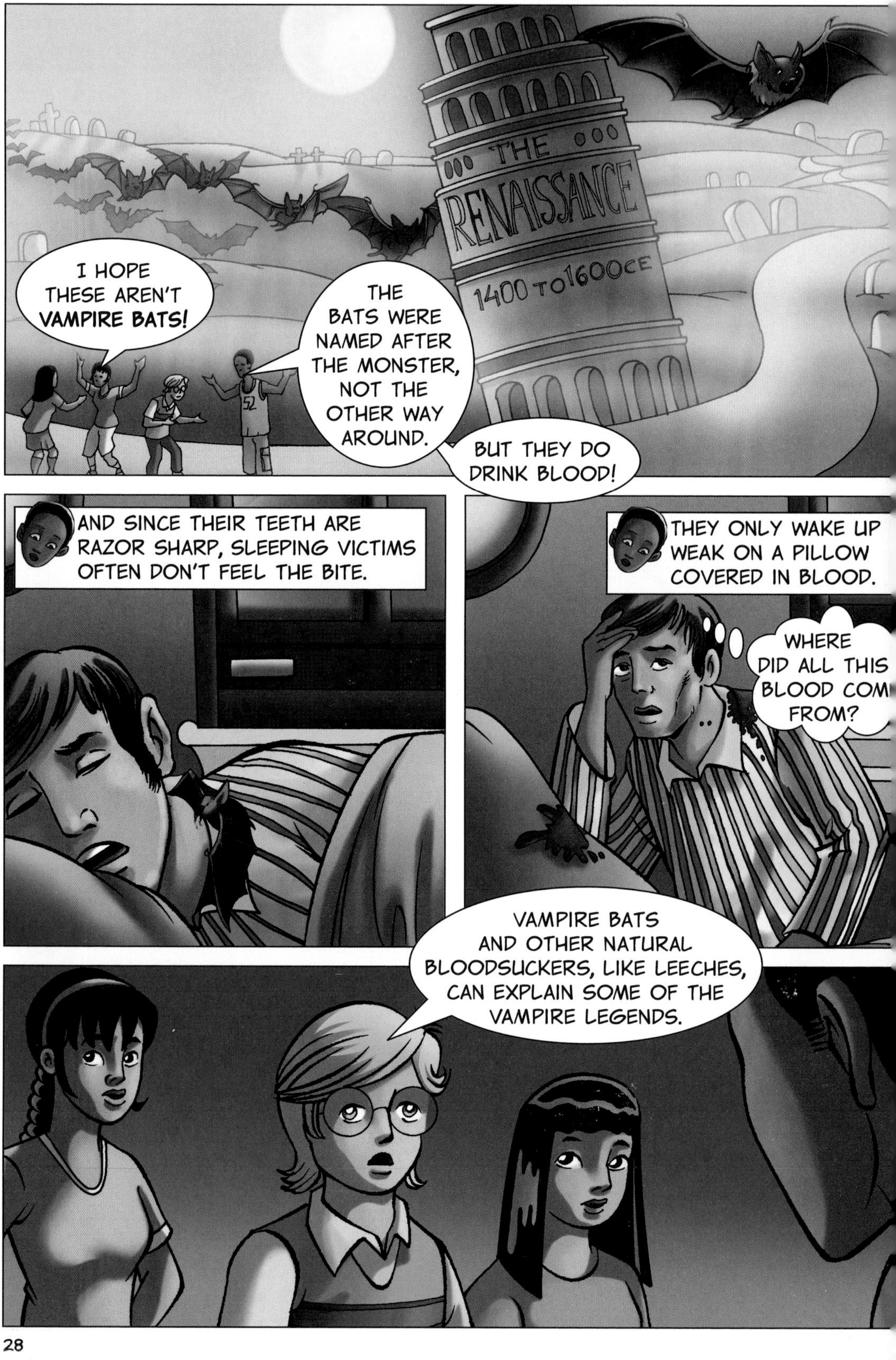
THE RENAISSANCE
1400 TO 1600 CE
I HOPE THESE AREN'T **VAMPIRE BATS!**
THE BATS WERE NAMED AFTER THE MONSTER, NOT THE OTHER WAY AROUND.
BUT THEY DO DRINK BLOOD!
AND SINCE THEIR TEETH ARE RAZOR SHARP, SLEEPING VICTIMS OFTEN DON'T FEEL THE BITE.
THEY ONLY WAKE UP WEAK ON A PILLOW COVERED IN BLOOD.
WHERE DID ALL THIS BLOOD COM FROM?
VAMPIRE BATS AND OTHER NATURAL BLOODSUCKERS, LIKE LEECHES, CAN EXPLAIN SOME OF THE VAMPIRE LEGENDS.

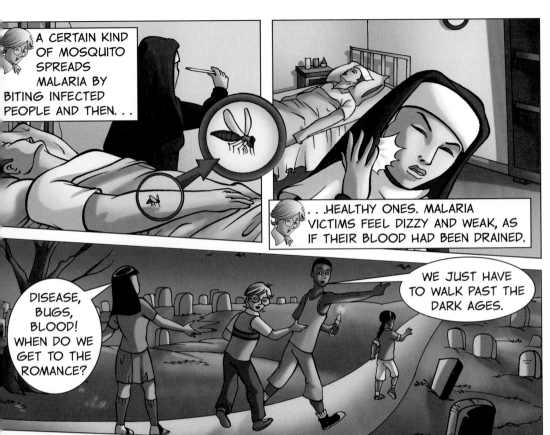

A CERTAIN KIND OF MOSQUITO SPREADS MALARIA BY BITING INFECTED PEOPLE AND THEN. . .

. . .HEALTHY ONES. MALARIA VICTIMS FEEL DIZZY AND WEAK, AS IF THEIR BLOOD HAD BEEN DRAINED.

DISEASE, BUGS, BLOOD! WHEN DO WE GET TO THE ROMANCE?

WE JUST HAVE TO WALK PAST THE DARK AGES.

THE ENLIGHTENMENT 1700 TO 1800 CE

WILL WE REACH THE TRIUMPH OF SCIENCE OVER SUPERSTITION SOON?

BE PATIENT. IN THE 18TH CENTURY, LOTS OF PEOPLE STILL BELIEVED IN VAMPIRES.

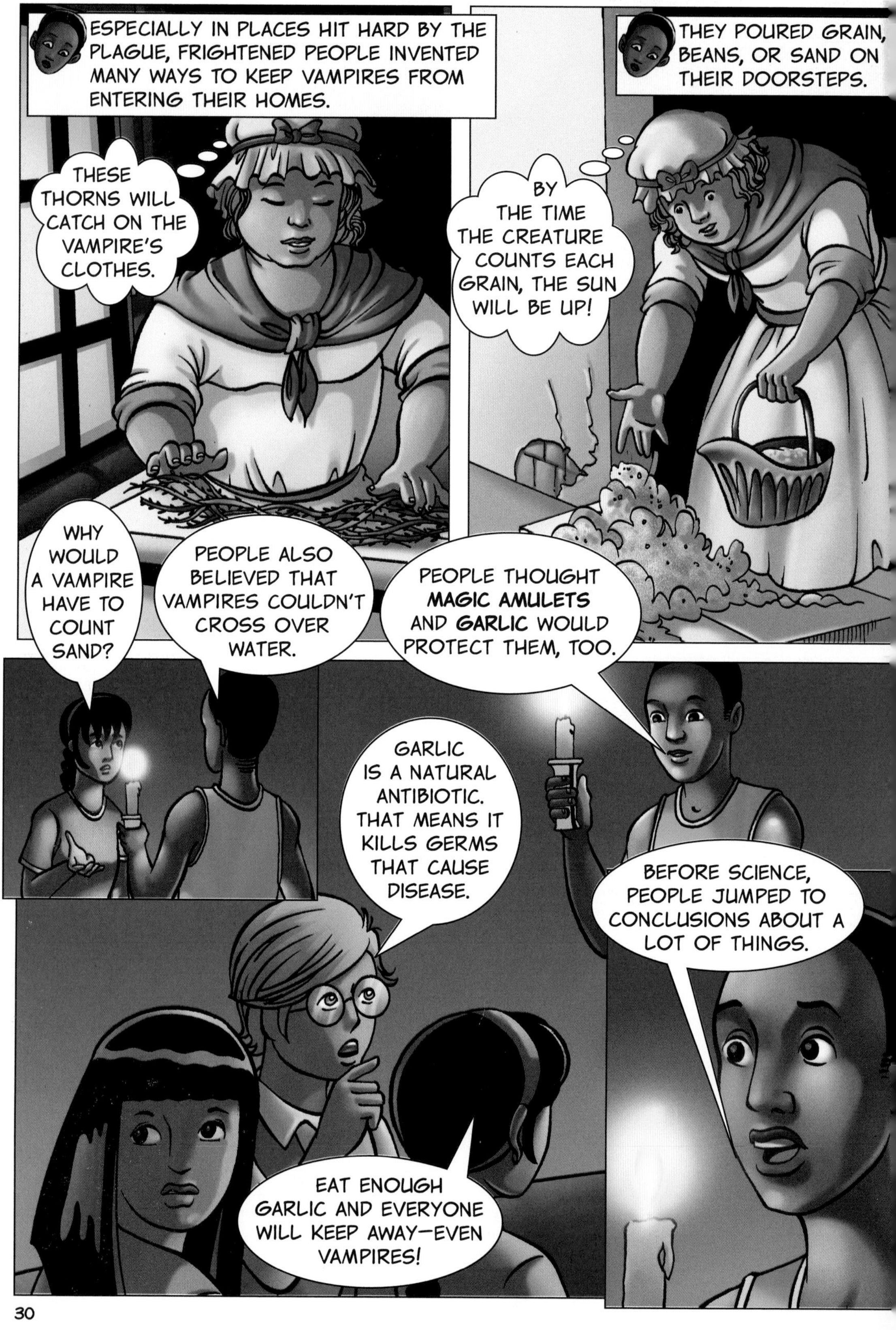
ESPECIALLY IN PLACES HIT HARD BY THE PLAGUE, FRIGHTENED PEOPLE INVENTED MANY WAYS TO KEEP VAMPIRES FROM ENTERING THEIR HOMES.
THESE THORNS WILL CATCH ON THE VAMPIRE'S CLOTHES.
THEY POURED GRAIN, BEANS, OR SAND ON THEIR DOORSTEPS.
BY THE TIME THE CREATURE COUNTS EACH GRAIN, THE SUN WILL BE UP!
WHY WOULD A VAMPIRE HAVE TO COUNT SAND?
PEOPLE ALSO BELIEVED THAT VAMPIRES COULDN'T CROSS OVER WATER.
PEOPLE THOUGHT **MAGIC AMULETS** AND **GARLIC** WOULD PROTECT THEM, TOO.
GARLIC IS A NATURAL ANTIBIOTIC. THAT MEANS IT KILLS GERMS THAT CAUSE DISEASE.
BEFORE SCIENCE, PEOPLE JUMPED TO CONCLUSIONS ABOUT A LOT OF THINGS.
EAT ENOUGH GARLIC AND EVERYONE WILL KEEP AWAY—EVEN VAMPIRES!

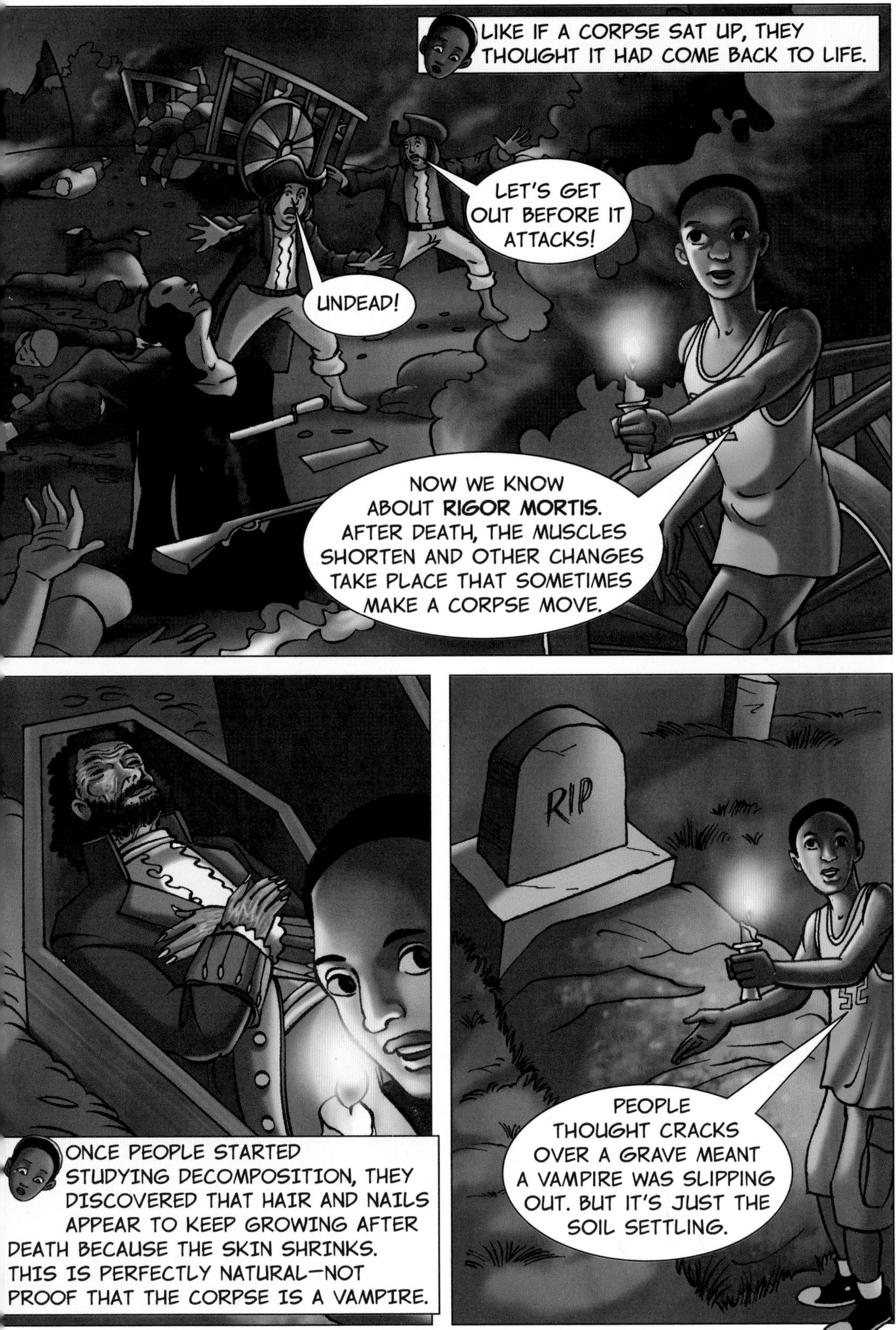
LIKE IF A CORPSE SAT UP, THEY THOUGHT IT HAD COME BACK TO LIFE.
LET'S GET OUT BEFORE IT ATTACKS!
UNDEAD!
NOW WE KNOW ABOUT **RIGOR MORTIS.** AFTER DEATH, THE MUSCLES SHORTEN AND OTHER CHANGES TAKE PLACE THAT SOMETIMES MAKE A CORPSE MOVE.
ONCE PEOPLE STARTED STUDYING DECOMPOSITION, THEY DISCOVERED THAT HAIR AND NAILS APPEAR TO KEEP GROWING AFTER DEATH BECAUSE THE SKIN SHRINKS. THIS IS PERFECTLY NATURAL—NOT PROOF THAT THE CORPSE IS A VAMPIRE.
RIP
PEOPLE THOUGHT CRACKS OVER A GRAVE MEANT A VAMPIRE WAS SLIPPING OUT. BUT IT'S JUST THE SOIL SETTLING.

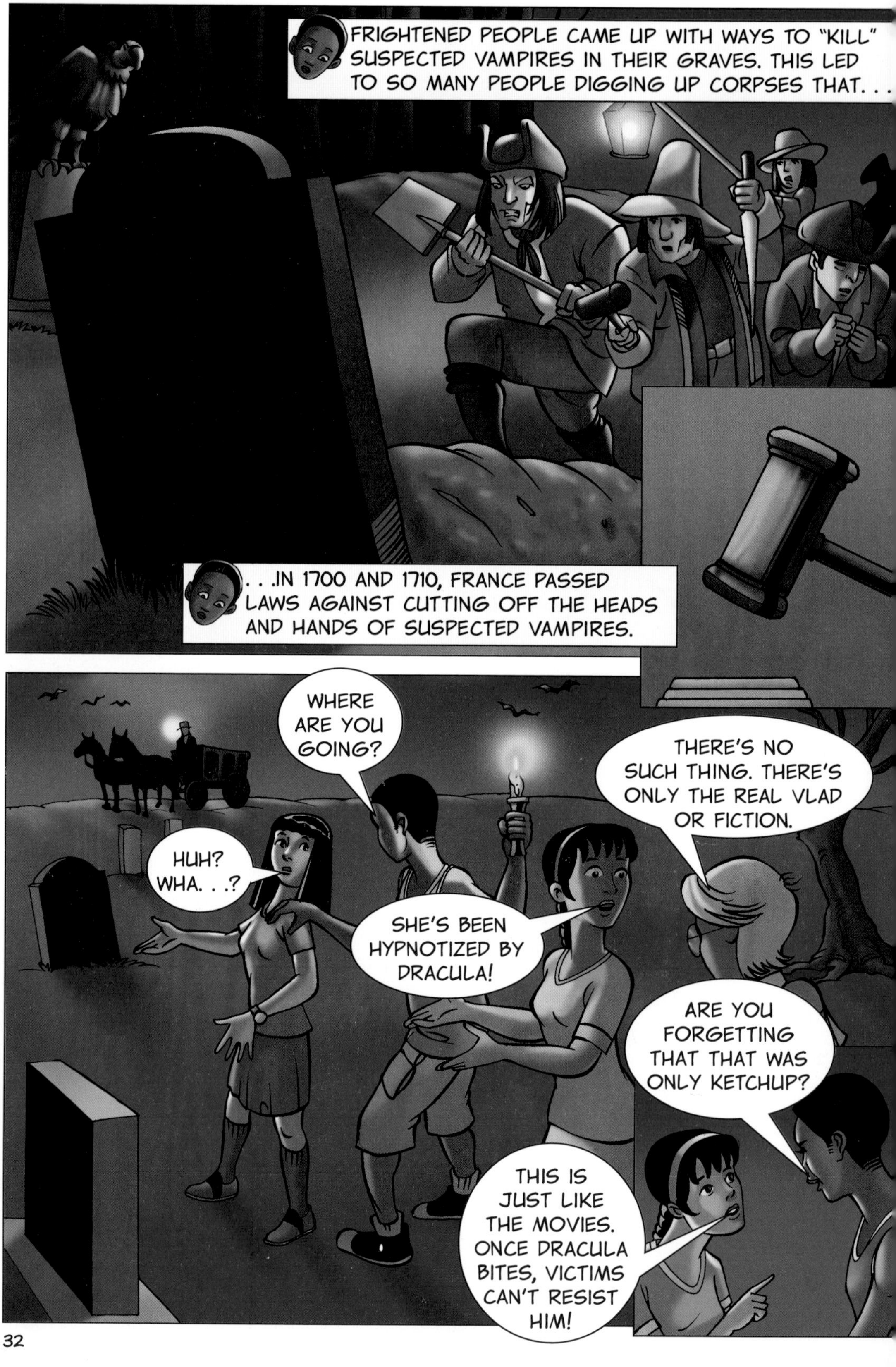
FRIGHTENED PEOPLE CAME UP WITH WAYS TO "KILL" SUSPECTED VAMPIRES IN THEIR GRAVES. THIS LED TO SO MANY PEOPLE DIGGING UP CORPSES THAT. . .
. . .IN 1700 AND 1710, FRANCE PASSED LAWS AGAINST CUTTING OFF THE HEADS AND HANDS OF SUSPECTED VAMPIRES.
WHERE ARE YOU GOING?
HUH? WHA. . .?
SHE'S BEEN HYPNOTIZED BY DRACULA!
THERE'S NO SUCH THING. THERE'S ONLY THE REAL VLAD OR FICTION.
THIS IS JUST LIKE THE MOVIES. ONCE DRACULA BITES, VICTIMS CAN'T RESIST HIM!
ARE YOU FORGETTING THAT THAT WAS ONLY KETCHUP?

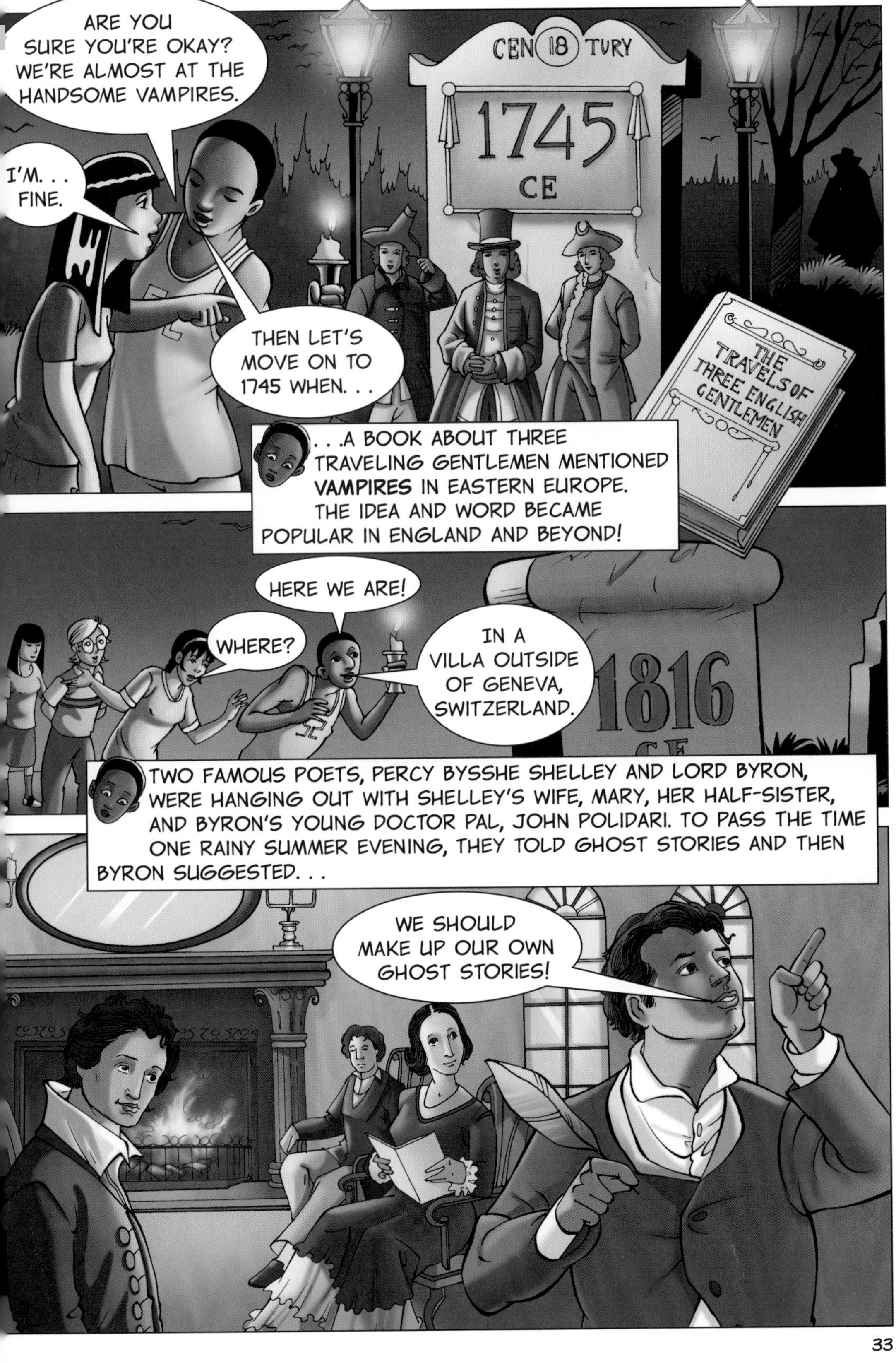
ARE YOU SURE YOU'RE OKAY? WE'RE ALMOST AT THE HANDSOME VAMPIRES.
I'M. . . FINE.
CEN 18 TURY
1745 CE
THEN LET'S MOVE ON TO 1745 WHEN. . .
THE TRAVELS OF THREE ENGLISH GENTLEMEN
. . .A BOOK ABOUT THREE TRAVELING GENTLEMEN MENTIONED **VAMPIRES** IN EASTERN EUROPE. THE IDEA AND WORD BECAME POPULAR IN ENGLAND AND BEYOND!
HERE WE ARE!
WHERE?
IN A VILLA OUTSIDE OF GENEVA, SWITZERLAND.
1816
TWO FAMOUS POETS, PERCY BYSSHE SHELLEY AND LORD BYRON, WERE HANGING OUT WITH SHELLEY'S WIFE, MARY, HER HALF-SISTER, AND BYRON'S YOUNG DOCTOR PAL, JOHN POLIDARI. TO PASS THE TIME ONE RAINY SUMMER EVENING, THEY TOLD GHOST STORIES AND THEN BYRON SUGGESTED. . .
WE SHOULD MAKE UP OUR OWN GHOST STORIES!

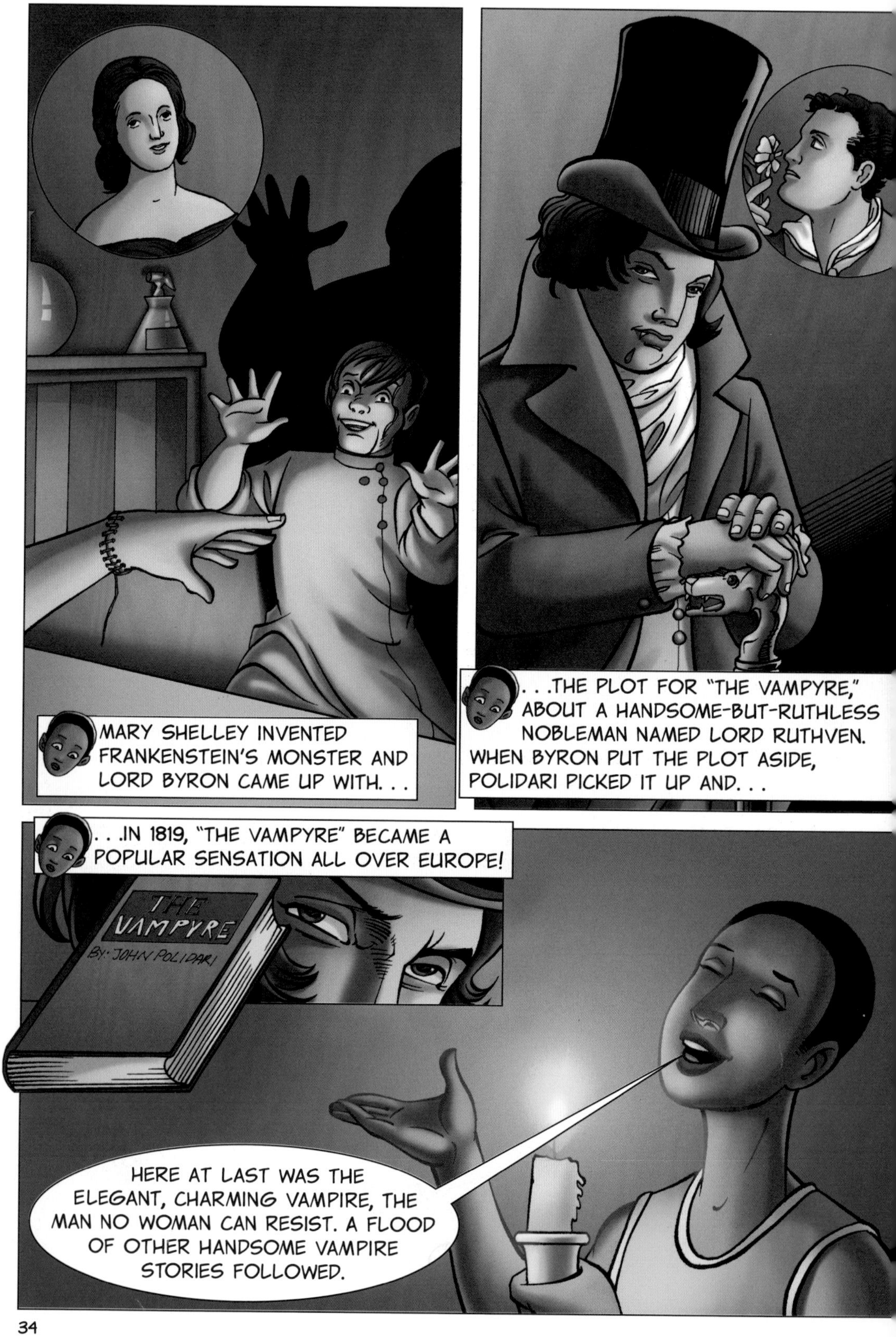
MARY SHELLEY INVENTED FRANKENSTEIN'S MONSTER AND LORD BYRON CAME UP WITH. . .
. . .THE PLOT FOR "THE VAMPYRE," ABOUT A HANDSOME-BUT-RUTHLESS NOBLEMAN NAMED LORD RUTHVEN. WHEN BYRON PUT THE PLOT ASIDE, POLIDARI PICKED IT UP AND. . .
. . .IN 1819, "THE VAMPYRE" BECAME A POPULAR SENSATION ALL OVER EUROPE!
THE VAMPYRE
BY: JOHN POLIDARI
HERE AT LAST WAS THE ELEGANT, CHARMING VAMPIRE, THE MAN NO WOMAN CAN RESIST. A FLOOD OF OTHER HANDSOME VAMPIRE STORIES FOLLOWED.

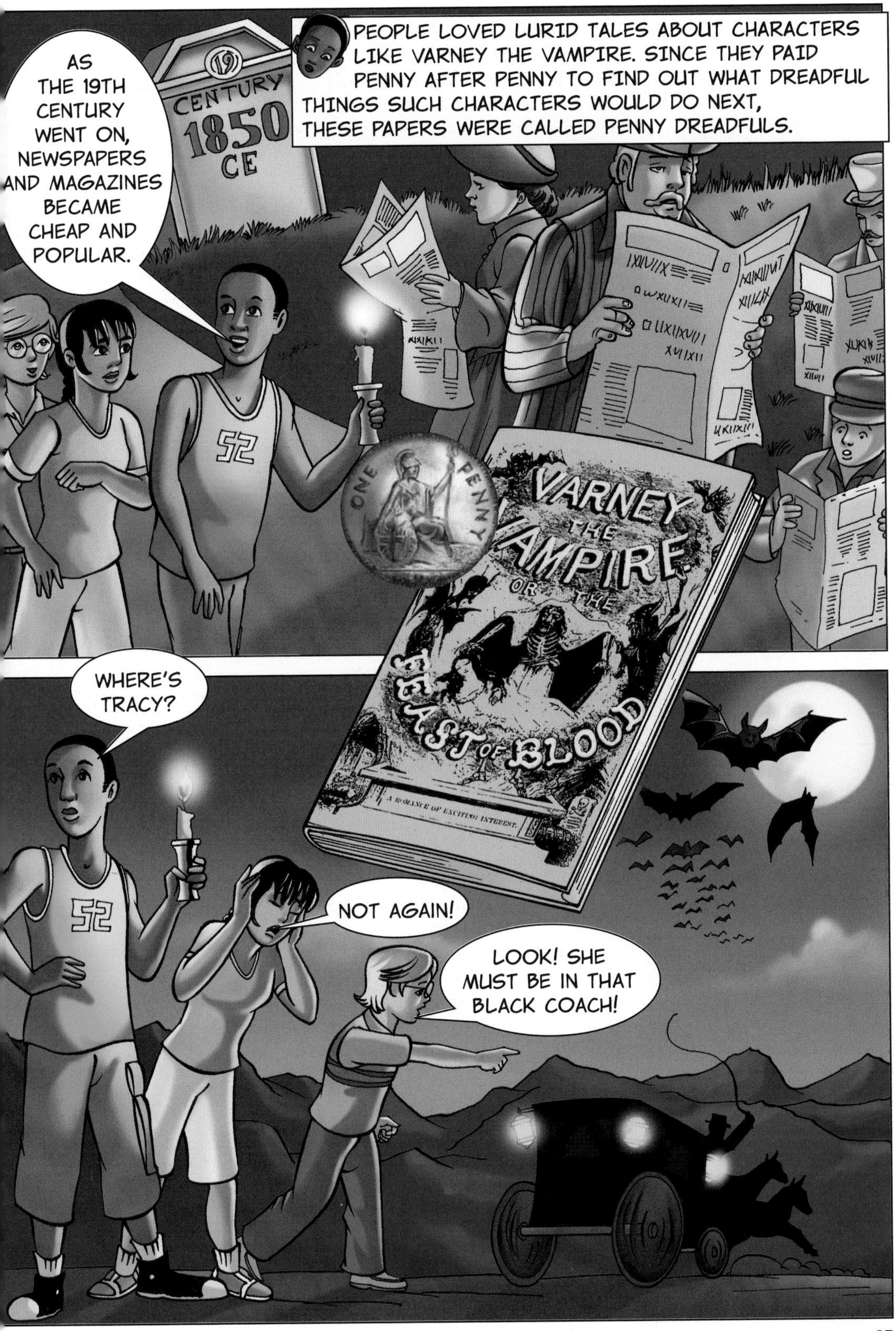
AS THE 19TH CENTURY WENT ON, NEWSPAPERS AND MAGAZINES BECAME CHEAP AND POPULAR.
PEOPLE LOVED LURID TALES ABOUT CHARACTERS LIKE VARNEY THE VAMPIRE. SINCE THEY PAID PENNY AFTER PENNY TO FIND OUT WHAT DREADFUL THINGS SUCH CHARACTERS WOULD DO NEXT, THESE PAPERS WERE CALLED PENNY DREADFULS.
19 CENTURY 1850 CE
ONE PENNY
VARNEY THE VAMPIRE OR THE FEAST OF BLOOD
A ROMANCE OF EXCITING INTEREST.
WHERE'S TRACY?
NOT AGAIN!
LOOK! SHE MUST BE IN THAT BLACK COACH!

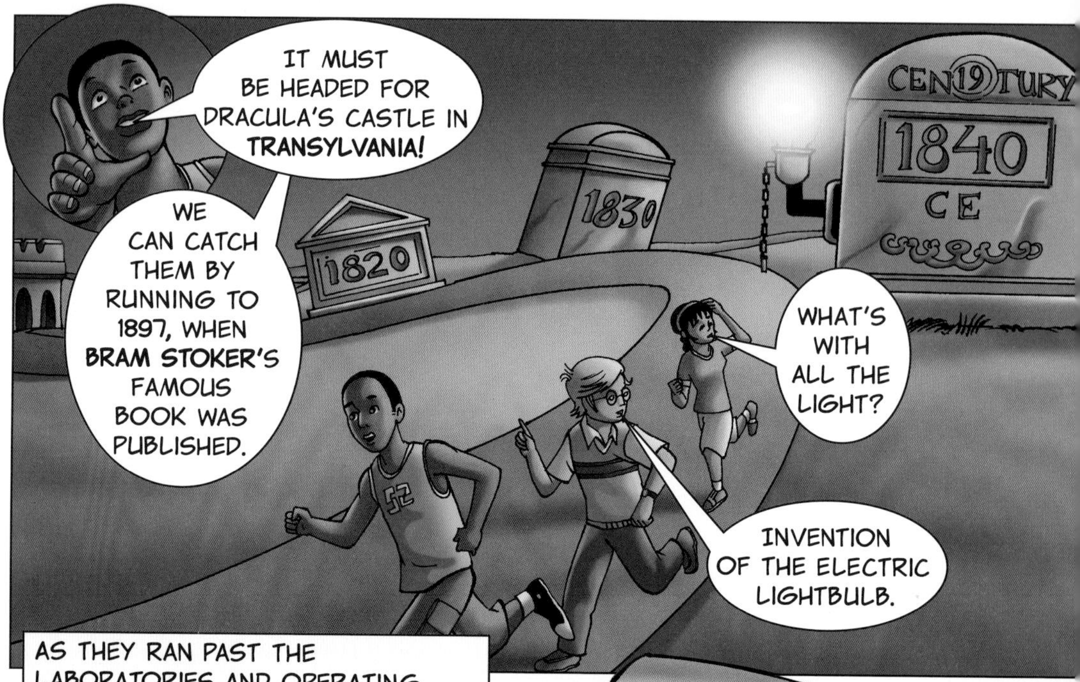
IT MUST BE HEADED FOR DRACULA'S CASTLE IN **TRANSYLVANIA!**
WE CAN CATCH THEM BY RUNNING TO 1897, WHEN **BRAM STOKER**'S FAMOUS BOOK WAS PUBLISHED.
1820
1830
CEN19TURY
1840
CE
WHAT'S WITH ALL THE LIGHT?
INVENTION OF THE ELECTRIC LIGHTBULB.

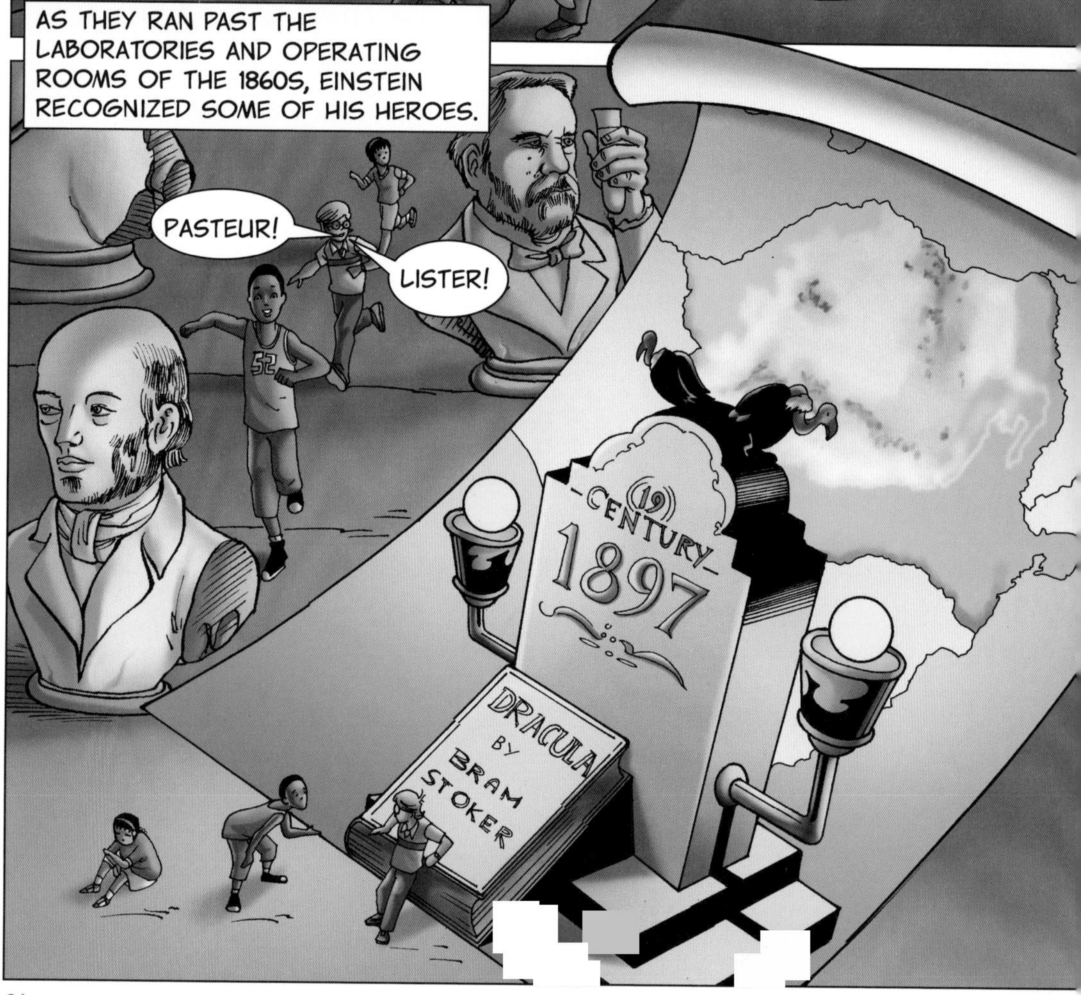
AS THEY RAN PAST THE LABORATORIES AND OPERATING ROOMS OF THE 1860S, EINSTEIN RECOGNIZED SOME OF HIS HEROES.
PASTEUR!
LISTER!
19 CENTURY
1897
DRACULA
BY
BRAM STOKER

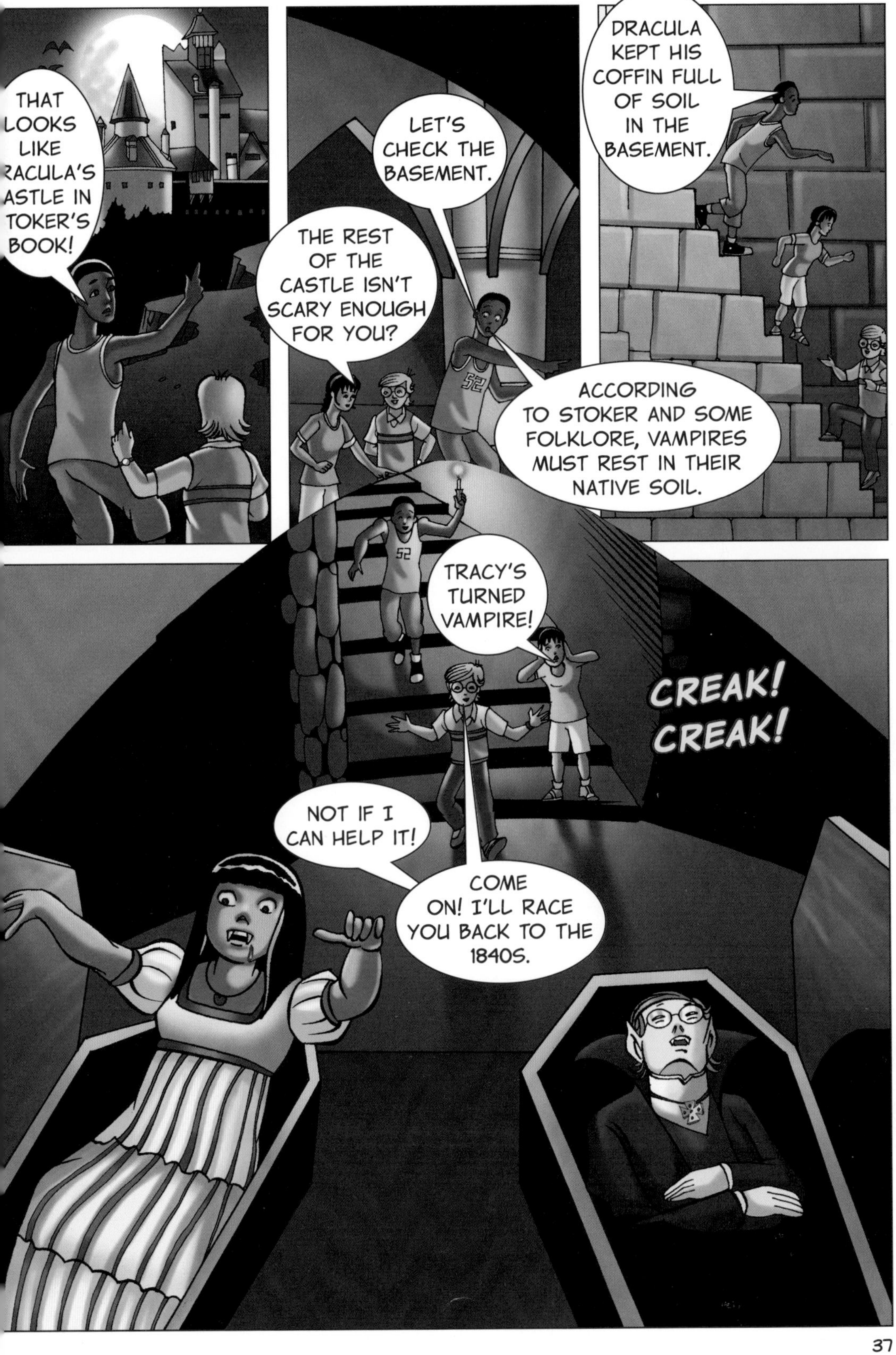
THAT LOOKS LIKE RACULA'S ASTLE IN TOKER'S BOOK!
LET'S CHECK THE BASEMENT.
THE REST OF THE CASTLE ISN'T SCARY ENOUGH FOR YOU?
DRACULA KEPT HIS COFFIN FULL OF SOIL IN THE BASEMENT.
ACCORDING TO STOKER AND SOME FOLKLORE, VAMPIRES MUST REST IN THEIR NATIVE SOIL.
TRACY'S TURNED VAMPIRE!
CREAK! CREAK!
NOT IF I CAN HELP IT!
COME ON! I'LL RACE YOU BACK TO THE 1840S.

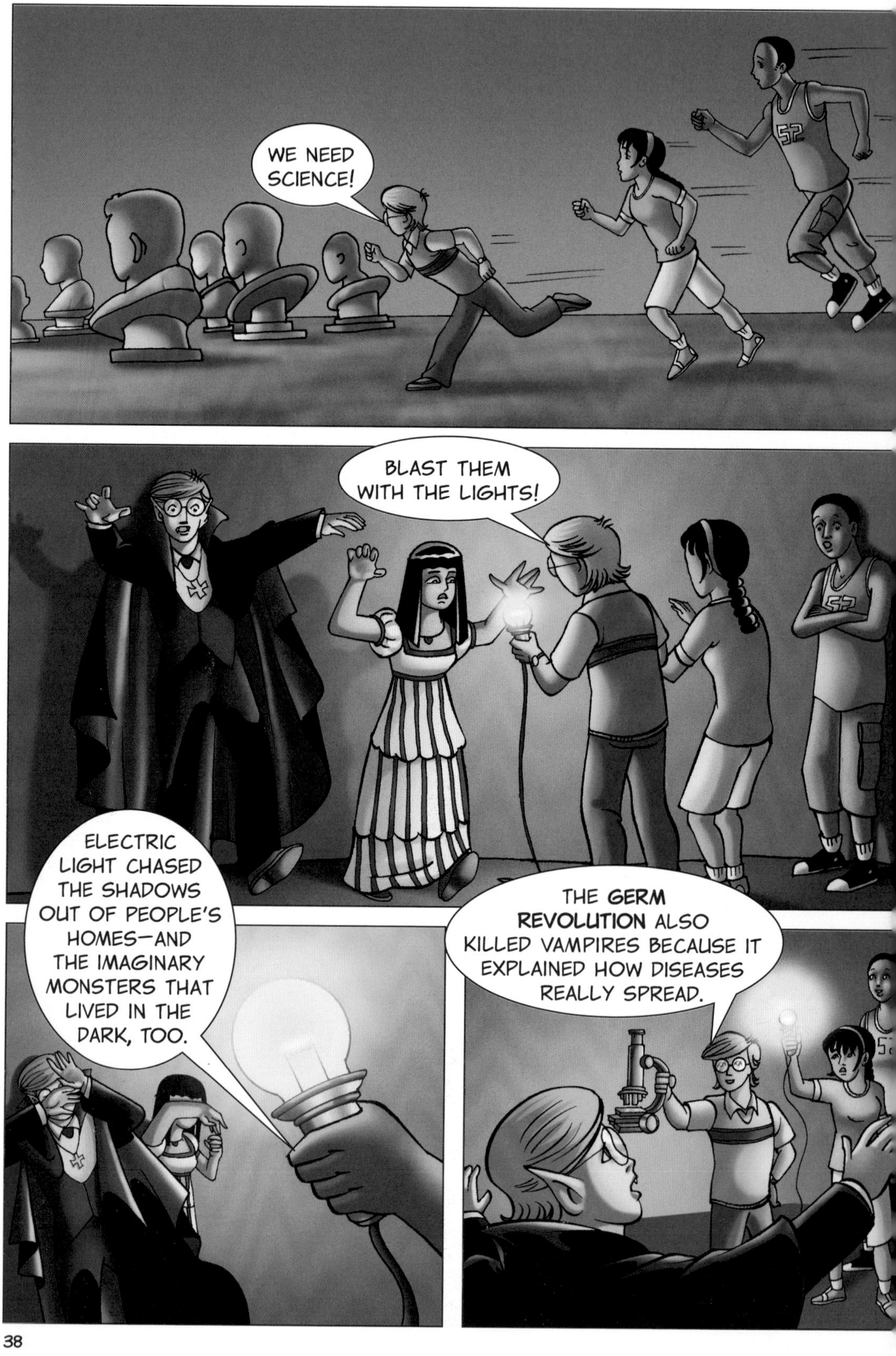
WE NEED SCIENCE!
BLAST THEM WITH THE LIGHTS!
ELECTRIC LIGHT CHASED THE SHADOWS OUT OF PEOPLE'S HOMES—AND THE IMAGINARY MONSTERS THAT LIVED IN THE DARK, TOO.
THE **GERM REVOLUTION** ALSO KILLED VAMPIRES BECAUSE IT EXPLAINED HOW DISEASES REALLY SPREAD.

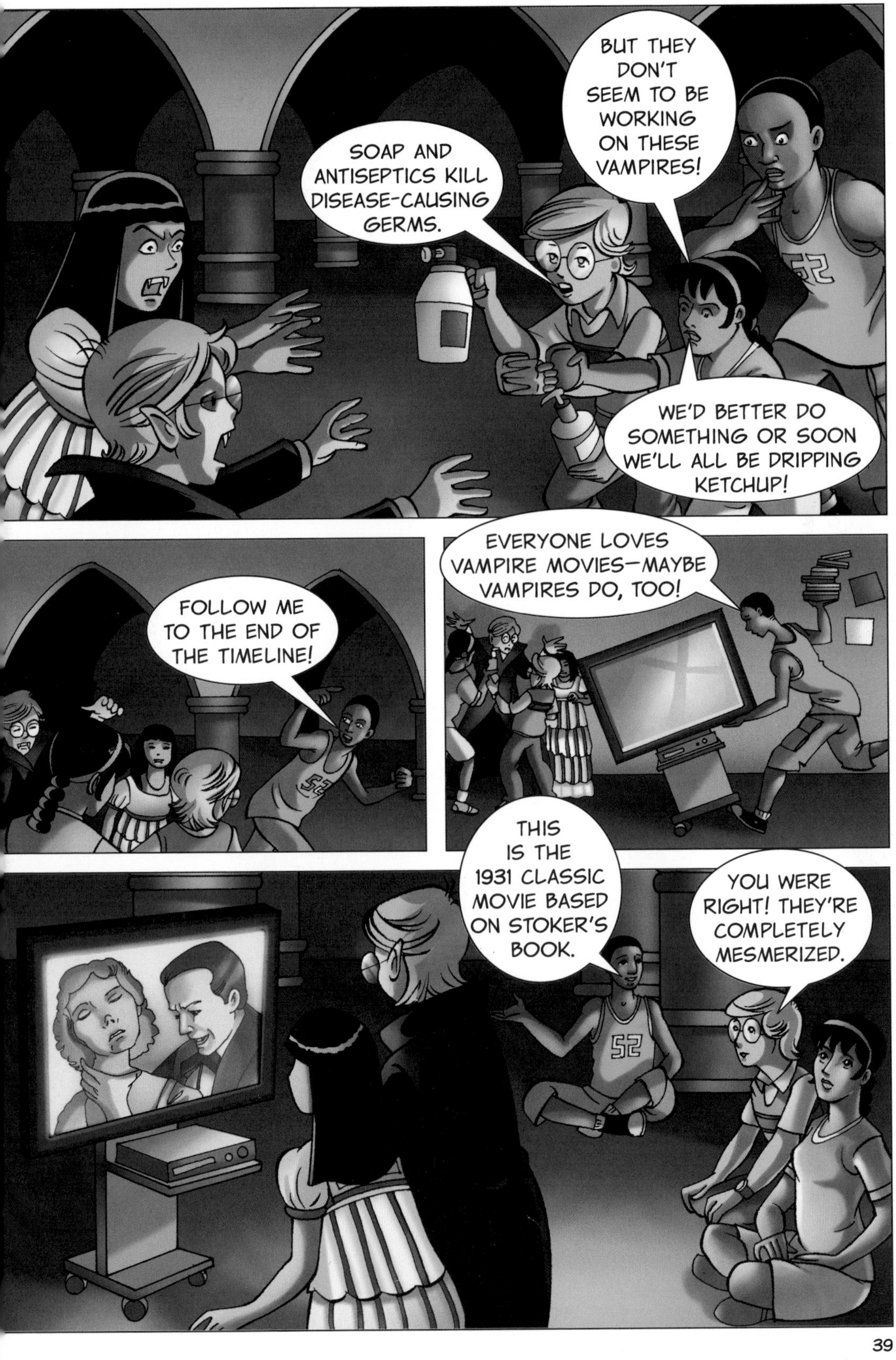
SOAP AND ANTISEPTICS KILL DISEASE-CAUSING GERMS.
BUT THEY DON'T SEEM TO BE WORKING ON THESE VAMPIRES!
WE'D BETTER DO SOMETHING OR SOON WE'LL ALL BE DRIPPING KETCHUP!
FOLLOW ME TO THE END OF THE TIMELINE!
EVERYONE LOVES VAMPIRE MOVIES—MAYBE VAMPIRES DO, TOO!
THIS IS THE 1931 CLASSIC MOVIE BASED ON STOKER'S BOOK.
YOU WERE RIGHT! THEY'RE COMPLETELY MESMERIZED.

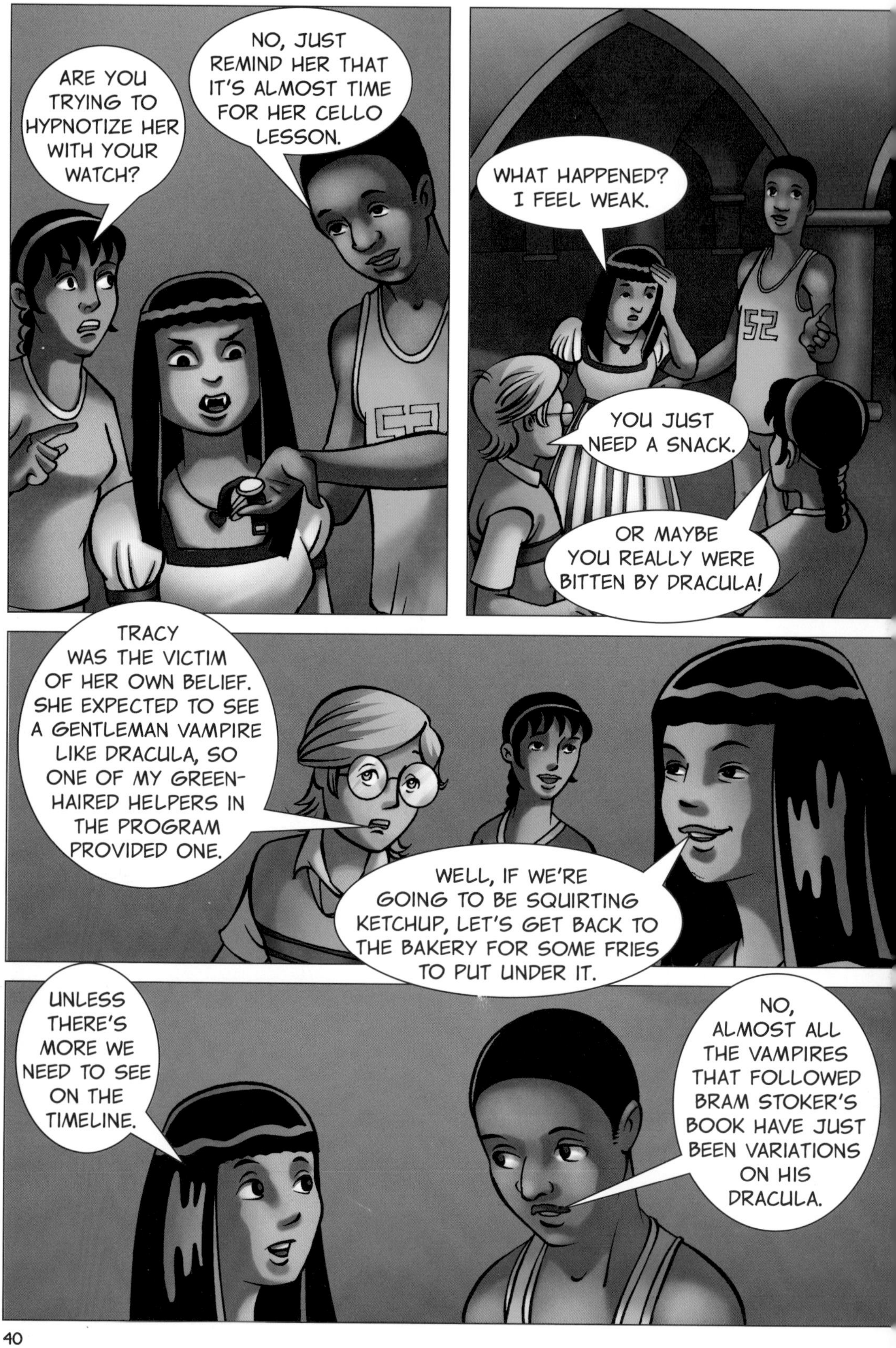
ARE YOU TRYING TO HYPNOTIZE HER WITH YOUR WATCH?
NO, JUST REMIND HER THAT IT'S ALMOST TIME FOR HER CELLO LESSON.
WHAT HAPPENED? I FEEL WEAK.
YOU JUST NEED A SNACK.
OR MAYBE YOU REALLY WERE BITTEN BY DRACULA!
TRACY WAS THE VICTIM OF HER OWN BELIEF. SHE EXPECTED TO SEE A GENTLEMAN VAMPIRE LIKE DRACULA, SO ONE OF MY GREEN-HAIRED HELPERS IN THE PROGRAM PROVIDED ONE.
WELL, IF WE'RE GOING TO BE SQUIRTING KETCHUP, LET'S GET BACK TO THE BAKERY FOR SOME FRIES TO PUT UNDER IT.
UNLESS THERE'S MORE WE NEED TO SEE ON THE TIMELINE.
NO, ALMOST ALL THE VAMPIRES THAT FOLLOWED BRAM STOKER'S BOOK HAVE JUST BEEN VARIATIONS ON HIS DRACULA.

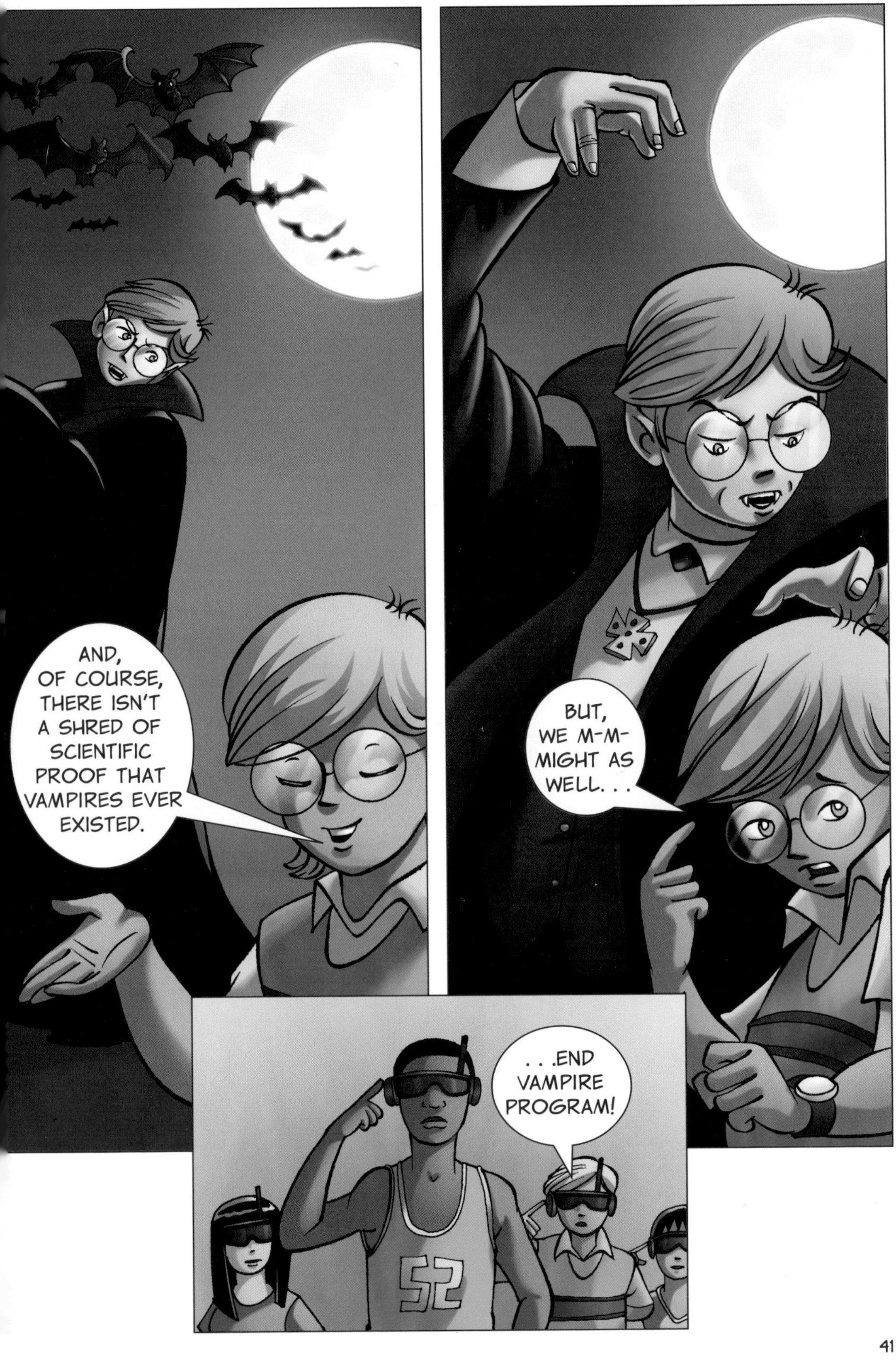
AND, OF COURSE, THERE ISN'T A SHRED OF SCIENTIFIC PROOF THAT VAMPIRES EVER EXISTED.
BUT, WE M-M-MIGHT AS WELL. . .
. . .END VAMPIRE PROGRAM!
52

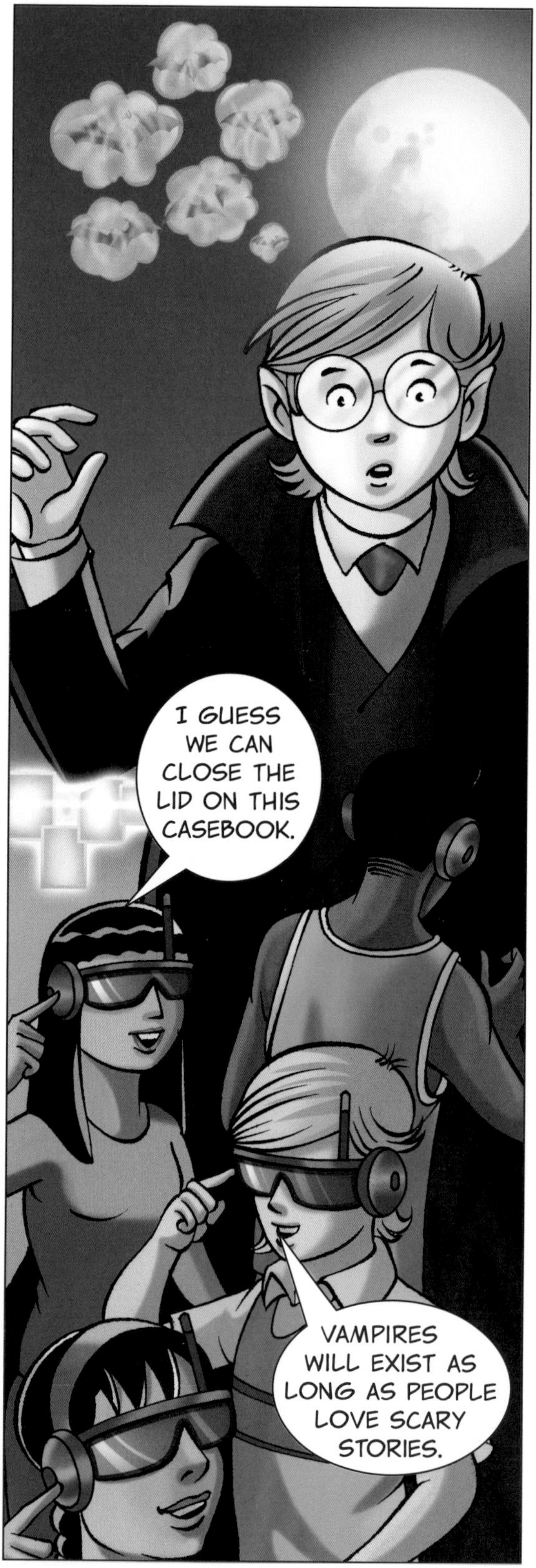
I GUESS WE CAN CLOSE THE LID ON THIS CASEBOOK.
VAMPIRES WILL EXIST AS LONG AS PEOPLE LOVE SCARY STORIES.

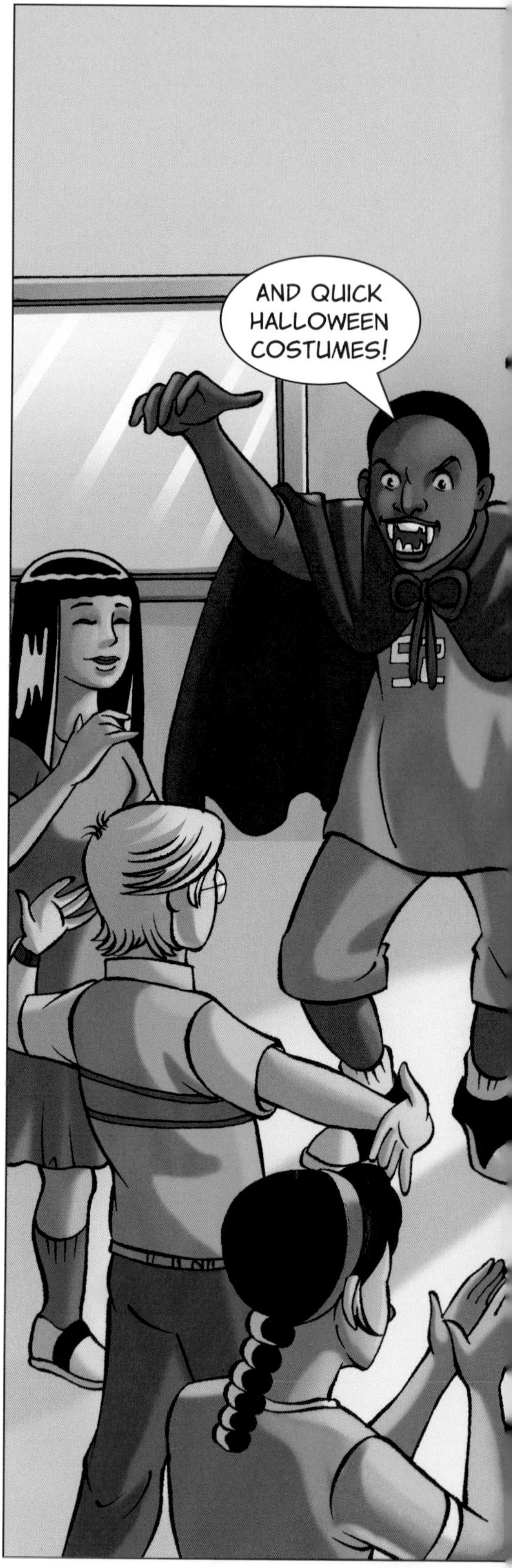
AND QUICK HALLOWEEN COSTUMES!

FACT FILE

Zombie: From the West African *zumbi,* meaning "fetish," which is an object supposed to have magic powers or to be inhabited by a spirit. A zombie is a corpse said to be revived by witchcraft. The word is also used to describe a dull person.

Superstition: A belief in the supernatural; an unreasonable fear of the unknown; a practice, opinion, or religion based on the above; a widely-held but false idea of the effects or nature of a thing.

Demon: From the Latin *daemon,* which is from the Greek *daimon,* meaning "deity," which is a god or goddess. An evil spirit or devil, especially one thought to possess a person; the personification of evil; a mean supernatural being; a cruel or destructive person.

FACT FILE

Cremate: From the Latin *cremare* meaning "to burn" or "to consume (a corpse, etc.) by fire." Cremation requires extremely hot temperatures to completely burn bones and organs like the heart.

Malaria: From the Italian *mal'aria* meaning "bad air." A recurring fever caused by a tiny parasite introduced by the bite of a mosquito. Since mosquitoes breed in the stagnant water of swamps and marshes, people associated malaria with bad air.

Rigor mortis: These two Latin words mean "the stiffness of death." Rigor mortis describes the changes that occur in a body after death, including the drying out of muscle tissues that may cause a corpse to sit up.

FACT FILE

Decompose: From the French *decomposer* meaning "to decay," "to rot," or "to separate into its elements or simpler parts;" to break down or spoil; to come apart. Decomposition happens to all living things after they die.

Transylvania: The region of Eastern Europe that was the birthplace of Vlad the Impaler and many vampire legends. Early travelers gave it the name, which combines the prefix *trans* meaning "across", "over," or "beyond" and *silva*, the Latin word for "forest" because to reach Transylvania, travelers must go over the Carpathian Mountains, which are thickly covered with trees. The region includes modern Romania and parts of Hungary, Serbia, and Ukraine.

Germ revolution: The giant change in medical theory that took place between 1879 and 1900, based on the discoveries of scientists like Louis Pasteur and Joseph Lister, who helped uncover the tiny organisms that cause disease. Before the germ revolution, people believed illnesses were caused by evil spirits, vampires, or other supernatural things.

Find Out for Yourself

Be like Lord Byron! Gather a group of friends to make up stories about vampires or to learn about some of the subjects Frank didn't cover in his casebook.

• Vampires from around the world, including Chinese *chiang-shih*, Malaysian *Penanggalen*, ancient Greek Lamia, and ancient Hebrew Lilith.

• Shape shifting and vampires.

• The germ revolution: How Pasteur, Lister, and others changed the way people fight disease.

• Nature's vampires, parasitic plants, and animals.

Web Sites

To ensure the currency and safety of recommended Internet links, Windmill maintains and updates an online list of sites related to the subject of this book. To access this list of web sites, please go to

www.windmillbks.com/weblinks

and select this book's title.

About the Author/Artist

Justine and Ron Fontes met at a publishing house in New York City, where he worked for the comic book department and she was an editorial assistant in children's books. Together, they have written over 500 children's books, in every format from board books to historical novels. They live in Maine, where they continue their work in writing and comics and publish a newsletter, *critter news*.

For more great fiction and nonfiction, go to www.windmillbooks.com